THE TOURIST'S GUIDE TO
HAUNTED WELLMAN

JAMES A. MOORE
AND
CHARLES R. RUTLEDGE

Introduction

Juggling Knives:
Collaborating with James A. Moore

"I didn't know you wrote," Jim Moore said to me one night in 2011. It was shortly after Jim's first wife Bonnie had passed away, and Jim had started joining me and a group of friends who met for dinner every Wednesday night. I'd known Jim for years, and knew he was a published author, but we hadn't really spent that much time together at that point. I'd just had a short story published and was telling the gang about it. Jim asked me to send him the story, so I did.

The next week at dinner, Jim said, "You can write. We should write a book together." That was James A. Moore. I had written and sold one short story, so obviously I could write a novel with him. I said as much, but Jim assured me I'd do fine. Then he told me he was talking to a publisher about a novel that would combine horror with crime fiction and from our dinner conversations he knew I was a big reader of crime and mystery and had been for several decades. Thus, he figured I was the perfect guy to write the book with.

It took about another week before I determined he was serious, but finally I said, okay, we'll write a book. Jim said, "Great. You start."

At that point Jim had written a couple dozen or so novels, so I was like, sure, you want the guy who never wrote a book before to start, but I dutifully sat down and hammered out the first chapter of what would become *Blind Shadows*. Then I wrote it again before sending it to Jim. When I got up the next morning, Jim had written chapter two and emailed it to me.

I was amazed at how quickly he sent the chapter back, but I wrote chapter three and sent it off. Chapter four came back the next day. And so it went for the next eight weeks. We finished the book and the publisher bought it, and just like that, I was a novelist. I wasn't aware at the time that Jim had a reputation for being an extremely fast writer, but then so am I. I just assumed all writers worked that way. Later Jim would gleefully tell people I was one of the few writers who could keep up with him.

He liked to say that we worked with such speed and energy that our collaborations were like "juggling knives at one another". Our second book, *Congregations of the Dead*, was written in six weeks.

That was the beginning of a series of collaborations that would span more than a decade. Four more novels and several short stories would follow. When people would ask me what it was like collaborating with Jim, I always said it was like going to your best friend's house when you were nine and playing with G.I. Joes in the backyard. We always had a ridiculous amount of fun.

What is perhaps most amazing about our work is that neither of us liked to plot in advance, so we were quite literally making it up as we went along, but our imaginations were remarkably in sync. So much so that I could write half a short story, hand it over to Jim and he would finish it without us having discussed it. He actually stopped halfway through a sentence on one of our stories and I picked it up from there and wrote to the end.

One of the things Jim told me when we began *Blind Shadows* is "You have to leave your ego at the door to co-author a book". And we did. When we got each other's chapters, we would edit and rewrite as we went. When Jim wrote a Carl Price chapter that featured Wade Griffin, I would rewrite Griffin to sound the way I wanted, and he would do the same when I wrote Carl. Years later, I can't always tell who wrote what in our novels because often a paragraph, or even a sentence would contain words by both of us. It was a true collaboration.

Things got a little more complicated the last few years we worked together. Jim had branched out from horror fiction to write grimdark heroic fantasy. His *Seven Forges* books were well received, and he spent a lot of time working in that genre while still writing horror for other publishers. We were still doing short stories together, but deadlines for his other work made it harder for us to hammer out a novel on spec. And by that time I was a lot busier as a writer too.

The Tourist's Guide to Haunted Wellman began one Halloween when Jim and I went with some friends on a Ghost Tour of Marietta, Georgia. By the time the tour was over, we'd decided we would write a book about the urban legends of a small Georgia town. Since we had already established, in the Griffin and Price novels, that our imaginary city of Wellman, Georgia, had a history of supernatural occurrences, it made sense to set the book there.

Haunted Wellman was written over a period of about four years off and on, a far cry from our "juggling knives" days, but we were still having fun. Jonathan Crowley was in good form and my own occult detective, Carter Decamp, got the most "screentime" he'd ever received in a novel. During that period Jim and I still wrote several short stories together and talked constantly about new projects and ideas for the future.

But that was not to be. Jim's battle with cancer had entered its final stages in early 2024 and he never got a shot at a second draft of *Haunted Wellman*. But at least we finished the book, our last full collaboration. Right into Jim's last days we were still exchanging PMs online, talking about what we wanted to do next, though I suspect both of us knew that wasn't going to happen.

But enough of that. With *The Tourist's Guide to Haunted Wellman*, Jim and I hoped to write a true horror novel. I think we did, and I think it's a good sendoff for Jim's signature character, Jonathan Crowley. I hope you enjoy it, and I hope you can feel some of the fun we had writing it.

Charles R. Rutledge
Atlanta, Georgia. 2025

PART I

*B*rennert County, Georgia, is a beautiful place. Nestled in the north Georgia mountains, and only a little over an hour and a half away from Atlanta (depending on traffic, of course) the buildings in the area are a collection of traditional Southern homes and a few surprises. The area has been lived in for years, and the history is rich with tales of heroism and villainy alike. During the Civil War there were plenty of those tales to be told, and exactly who the bad guys were was often a matter of perspective.

Looking at the homes, landmarks, and lush green hills, you'd think that Brennert County, and towns like Wellman, were just about postcard perfect. But as is often the case in the South, there are things not mentioned, places not spoken of in polite society, that hold dark, and sometimes even dangerous, secrets.

Wellman, Georgia, and the surrounding areas are steeped in a history of violence, madness and murder. There are tragedies aplenty to go with the local legends of goblins, like the Moon-Eyes, and the tales of witches buried in the Hollow, or living in the places where the sun almost never shows itself. Wellman is a place where families have kept themselves for close to two hundred years, never leaving once they found the locations that felt like home to them. What could be better? What could possibly go wrong?

Read carefully and you'll learn of love lost, of murder most foul, of people hanged for crimes they did not commit and young lovers who died trying to save each other. Take the time to study this book and you'll discover where a man buried his own family in the walls, along with their fortune, to keep them all "safe" from invading forces, and you'll hear the truth about some of the Native American Mounds that even the Cherokee are afraid to go near. You'll hear tales of heroism and stories of dark deeds that were never punished. You'll learn where statues cry bloody tears and find out about the judge that took the law into his own hands and made sure the guilty were punished for crimes they thought they got away with.

You'll discover the road where a little girl wanders when the sun sets, looking for her family dog, and some say running from the man who murdered her and her family alike. You'll find out why the ghost of Ethan Crane still haunts the *one of the local churches and if the stories are true, still seeks the man who cut his eyes and heart from his body.*

There are tales of Confederate soldiers who wander along a dark road with plans to kill the Yankee conspirators who betrayed them, and legends of a battle that replays every hundred days, revealing the locations of where each person died and maybe even showing where treasure is buried if you pay attention to the clues.

All this and more await you in The Tourist's Guide to Haunted Wellman, *a book of stories meticulously studied and verified by the Brennert County Paranormal Society. We know what haunts you.*

———

"Are we really doing this?" Emily Strand looked at the rest of the society members and spoke softly, her voice barely carrying far enough for anyone to hear.

Travis Dunlap heard her, of course. Travis would have heard Emily from twice as far away and if she were whispering as softly as she could, because every word she said was very nearly holy in his mind. She owned his heart and he would marry her someday, if he ever got up the nerve to actually speak to her.

Don Washington was the one who answered her question, of course. Don, who was twenty-six and knew more about the supernatural than most of them, was the Vice President of the Brennert County Paranormal Society, and he was the driving force behind the book they'd been writing and the plans they had to make sure that the ghosts were really there.

Well, none of them were really writing the book, they had a ghostwriter. Travis snorted when he thought about that. A ghostwriter for a book of ghost stories. Of course, Don didn't think that was funny at all. Don took everything as seriously as a heart attack.

"Yes, for the tenth time, we're doing it, Emily. We have to make sure we're onto something. The book says we can prove the existence of ghosts just by reciting the right words, at the right time, and in the right place."

Don huffed and puffed and sighed. He was not in great shape, really. Okay, he was obese, as in carrying an extra person around his guts and butt. They'd been walking for close to a quarter mile and most everyone was just fine, but Don was wheezing and red-faced. Okay the clove cigarettes probably didn't help very much.

"I thought Charon said it was a bad idea." Emily really did whisper that time.

Don rolled his eyes and shook his jowly face. "Charon doesn't know everything. She's got a bookstore that sells occult crap and Tarot cards. Everything there is over-priced and a rip off. Have you seen the stupid books on local ghosts she has? Not even half as much stuff as we're including in our book." He hauled his pants back up to his waist as if that were a definitive statement about how foolish Charon was.

Travis grimaced. No one but Don thought poorly of Charon, and he only thought that way because she'd told him off about all the crazy experiments he wanted to do, like the one tonight. Charon's bookshop, Baba Yaga's, was over in Gatesville and was probably the best-stocked occult bookstore north of Atlanta. It was the primary reason she didn't have much time to spend with the group anymore.

Don had the wild idea of "enhancing" the ghostly experience by making the restless dead more restless. He said it was like agitating fireflies: harmless, but effective. To that end he'd used Ouija boards, a dozen different "rituals" he'd found online, and had even hunted down a few books that he said were supposed to "thin the barrier between the living and the land of the dead."

So far the only thing that had happened was they got to hang out together and wait, while nothing at all took place. Travis would have minded a lot more, but every time they got together for one of Don's experiments, he managed to sit as close as he could to Emily.

Emily, who was just about as perfect as any girl had ever been. He could count the freckles on her face a million times (there were exactly thirty-seven of them) and never get tired of it. Emily, who was so quiet and shy, even though she had the greatest eyes ever behind her glasses. Emily, who probably didn't even know his name, even though they went to school together and were in the society together. Emily, who thought Mark Irvin was about the cutest guy on the planet, if you judged the way she always looked at him.

He'd have hated Mark if the guy wasn't so damned nice.

"So that's a yes." Emily sighed and wrapped herself in her own arms to ward away the chill.

It *was* cold. Autumn was in the air, the sky was half buried in clouds, and the wind that blew through the area came from the north and west. There was frost on some of the trees and the grass under their feet crunched in a way it never did during the summer.

The First United Methodist Church on Maynard Avenue stood like a shadowed guardian over the area as they moved into the cemetery. The side of the building held hundreds of pumpkins set up for sale, even though the pastor there was not overly fond of Halloween. As they moved past the gate into the graveyard the bell at the church rang out eleven times, the sound so much louder in the night than it seemed when Travis was at home.

They passed the subject of one of the entries in the book, a life-size marble statue of a woman in a flowing robe. Travis didn't know if it was supposed to be the Virgin Mary or what, but local legend said that on full moons people had seen tears of blood in the statue's eyes, and heard the sounds of a woman weeping. They wound their way through the tombstones, many of those the unmarked graves of fallen Civil War soldiers, until they found the spot they were looking for.

Don let out another epic sigh and grunted as he lowered himself to the grass near the headstone of William Avery Harrington. The stone was rather unremarkable, but the dates showed that the old man had died at exactly one hundred years of age, down to the day. For the next fifteen minutes all of them sat around while Don looked over the things he'd brought with him and then he directed each of them to a different position as he started carefully making marks on the lawn with a bright white powder and then other marks in charcoal black.

It was ten minutes to midnight before he said he was ready. By then Travis had sidled closer to Emily and then slipped back when she moved over to talk to Mark, damn his eyes.

The mood was solemn and despite his appearance—unkempt on the best of days—Don lowered his voice and spoke clearly as he said the words written out on an old piece of parchment.

He finished at exactly midnight, as the bells of the church rang through the night air. The bells sounded wrong to Travis's ears.

They sounded angry.

Cindy Kane sat up from where she had been drowsing on her couch and put her hand to her forehead. She felt...something, but she couldn't identify it. A sudden release of emotion. Anger. But that didn't make sense. Cindy's abilities didn't work that way.

Cindy was a psychic, yes, but her talent was psychometry, the ability to divine information about people by touching objects that belonged to them. She didn't receive sudden psychic impressions, or at least she hadn't until now. That was more in her father's line. Cindy glanced at the clock. Midnight. *Well of course it was midnight.*

Whatever the feeling had been, it was gone now, but a kind of impression lingered. Call it psychic "bruising." She felt almost as if she had been struck a physical blow.

Cindy slid off the couch and went to her front door. She could feel cold air around the edges of the frame. She needed to speak to the apartment maintenance guys again about better insulating her door. She grabbed her jacket and stepped outside.

Cindy had been living near Gatesville State University for the last three months, since moving to Gatesville to work on her bachelor's degree at the college. She liked the area, though she was used to the hustle and bustle of downtown Atlanta, and Gatesville was a bit more rustic.

Cindy walked to the front steps of her building and stood at the top of the stairs. Stars wheeled overhead in the midnight sky and a cold wind rustled her jacket and stirred her hair. Cindy closed her eyes and tried to focus on what she had felt before. There was something, a wisp, a remnant of the feeling. She allowed it to turn her body.

When she stopped moving, she opened her eyes. She was facing north. Towards the Blue Ridge Mountains. Toward Wellman. Cindy gave a shudder that had little to do with the cold. She pulled her jacket closer, and went back inside to wait for dawn.

A moaning wind came up seemingly from nowhere, pulling at Travis's clothes. Don's carefully laid out dust patterns of chalk and charcoal went spinning into the autumn air.

"What the hell?" Don said, struggling to get his considerable bulk off the ground.

Travis heard a loud, cracking noise, and looking back at the tombstone of William Avery Harrington, he saw that the stone had broken in half. He took an involuntary step back. A longtime fan of horror movies, Travis half expected the moldering, skeletal form of Harrington to come lurching out of the grave.

But nothing happened. The wind fell off as the last echo of the final peal of the church bell faded.

"What did you do, Don?" Emily said.

Don said, "Hell if I know. But something happened."

"Whatever it was, it seems to be over," Mark said.

Travis noticed that Emily was clutching Mark and that he had his arm wrapped protectively around her. Travis gritted his teeth. Just then he thought he caught movement out of the corner of his eye, and he glanced toward it.

The statue was looking at him.

Or he thought it was. When they had passed the marble woman before, he'd have sworn she had been looking straight ahead. Now her face was turned slightly toward them. Maybe it was a trick of the light?

"Are you okay, Travis?" Emily said.

"Yeah. I guess all this kind of spooked me."

Mark dug into his jacket pocket and pulled out a small electromagnetic field detector. He held it over the broken tombstone. He said, "Nothing on the EMT."

Don rolled his eyes. "Like that means anything. You saw what happened. I got 'em riled up good."

Emily said, "I think we should go. Like Mark said, whatever happened, it seems to be over. We should go home and record what we saw."

"You guys can run home scared if you want," Don said.

"I don't think you should stay here alone, Don," Emily said.

"Hey, I'll be fine. I got all kinds of charms and stuff to protect me."

Travis said, "More things you got off the internet?"

Don's face reddened. He said, "Look Dunlap. I got more evidence of the existence of the supernatural tonight than you guys have found in months with your EMT devices and your laser thermometers. You're all just pissed because I got some results."

Mark said, "Come on, Travis. Emily. You know how he is when he gets like this."

"Gets like what, Mark?" Don said. "Huh? Gets like what?"

But Mark was already walking away, with Emily beside him. Travis said, "Come on, Don. Come with us."

"Just fuck off, Travis."

Travis threw up his hands and walked away. Mark was right. There was no reasoning with Don when he got this way. He hurried to catch up to Mark and Emily. Emily looked back over her shoulder, not at Travis but at the broken tombstone.

"Hey, don't do that Emily," Travis said.

"Do what?"

"Don't look back as you leave the cemetery. That's one of the oldest bits of folklore. Our ancestors wouldn't look back as they left a funeral. It was seen as an invitation for the departed to follow them home."

"That's just a legend, Travis," Emily said. But she wasn't smiling as she said it.

The Penobscot House

The Penobscot House sits at 17 Harvest Street, not far from the western edge of town. The house has a long history as a refuge for escaping slaves during the Civil War. According to a lot of old tales it was part of the Underground Railroad and slaves trying to get to the north and gain their freedom would move along that path and find a safe haven for a night or even longer.

But there are some people who say the truth was a lot darker than that. There are claims that Samuel Penobscot used the slaves that came through the area as his personal sex toys in some cases and experimented on them in others. The women slaves were captured and held for his pleasures. But the men, especially the younger men he deemed handsome or strong enough, were tortured and vivisectionalized.

There are accusations that Samuel Penobscot was a necromancer, a magician who deals with the dead. There are others who claim his work more closely resembled the fictional Victor Frankenstein's efforts.

Whatever the case, before and during the Civil War the stories allege that Penobscot experimented on over fifty slaves, killing them, or using them as his guinea pigs...or both.

According to a few stories the ghosts of those slaves still haunt the house and the surrounding properties, including the southern field where he allegedly buried the remains of his victims.

———

The Shallow Falls Apartments were situated in a nice little niche of land, just south of some of the older homes in Wellman. Each of the buildings held four units that were designed to accommodate as many as four people comfortably, with a large central living area and four smaller bedrooms that shared two and half baths. The cost of living there was not cheap, but four college kids could easily afford to split an apartment and survive the cost as long as they didn't go too crazy with the extras. Power and water were included in the rent. Cable and Wi-Fi were not.

When the buildings were built the land was swampy, to be kind, but careful work on the parts of the construction teams had found the source of the water and directed it to the "falls," a small reservoir that ran down to a pond carefully constructed away from the main building sites. At its deepest part the pond was roughly a foot and half down. Most nights in the summer a person couldn't escape the sounds of frogs burping and thrumming. The frogs were welcome as they kept down the mosquito populations. There were koi as well, but the fish often fell victim to a few hawks in the area.

The college kids didn't care. They fed the fish, they fed the frogs, they watched as the small pond froze over some winters and were shocked when the waters thawed and life came back to the area. None of which mattered in the least when Halloween was coming closer and there were parties to attend.

The party at Allison and Leo's place was not too loud, but it was moderately raucous just the same. There were twenty people there listening to techno-rap and playing their music of choice softly, because while a lot of college kids lived in the area, Howard Lindt also lived in the building and he'd call the cops any chance he could.

As there were several people imbibing in underage drinking and a few mind-altering substances, it was best to keep the police away.

Currently Allison was baked and giggling. Leo was sober and pretending to be offended by Allison's state of being. He was only pretending. They had a system. She got to party hard one time and he got to party hard the next. One of them was always sober and it was his turn. Anyone started getting unruly, they were escorted off the property as quickly as possible. It was a plan that normally kept things going smoothly.

Leo swept through the living room and took a cigarette from Troy Miller, who was currently drunk enough to set the couch on fire with his swinging butt. While the jock was trying to figure out where his cigarette had gone, Leo also confiscated his lighter and his pack.

Sometimes being a host was a trial, but Troy was cute, so he could forgive the man his sins as long as no actual puking took place.

The cigarettes went into Leo's personal stash. The lighter went into his pocket. He'd give it back the next day as it was an actual metal lighter with sentimental attachment.

He was just daydreaming about how much he wanted to get Troy in his bed when the flayed man walked through the wall of his living room and bled across the floor, the wall itself, and Leo.

Leo felt the hot blood spread across his arm and face as the flayed man touched him and screamed his agony out into the world around him. His dark eyes were round and wild, and his breath stank like a slaughterhouse. That might have just been the smell coming from his body, which had been peeled of skin as if he were a cucumber being readied for a salad.

The blood flowed freely, and the poor bastard's entire body shivered uncontrollably. Leo was an English major this year, but his first year he'd planned on being a nurse. He had seen enough pictures of burn victims and surgeries to know that what he was seeing wasn't a convincing fake.

The hand on his wrist still had some dark brown skin to it. The wrist was bared of any flesh. Blood soaked into Leo's white dress shirt—part of his Dracula outfit—and spread a crimson stain across his arm.

Leo had time to think about the pain the poor man must have been suffering later. At that moment all he could see was that a dying man was bleeding all over him. The reason he'd decided against being a nurse was painfully simple: blood terrified him.

Leo backed up, yanking his arm away, and screamed for all he was worth, his throat feeling as shredded as the flesh on the man who stumbled after him wailing in agony.

Leo pushed and pummeled the man, his voice breaking and his throat raw. Nevertheless, he screamed again and again as the bleeding man fell against the wall and then fell *through* it. Another massive bloodstain splattered along the eggshell-colored paint and slopped down to the thin gray carpeting in the hallway.

Leo turned and ran for the front room. His foot caught the end table in front of the communal couch, and he fell flat on his face. The impact stopped his screaming and knocked him unconscious, but not before Mr. Lindt called the police. The older neighbor didn't call about the party, or even Leo's screaming. He called about the naked, crying woman in his kitchen, who crawled on all fours and begged an unseen figure for mercy.

Howard Lindt did not see the person she begged, but he felt a presence. It was a malignant thing that haunted his dreams that night and the next several nights as well.

In his dreams he was raped and beaten, tortured and murdered, again and again.

A week later Lindt died of a massive coronary. The belief was that he died in his sleep and probably felt nothing.

The belief was very, very wrong.

Emily got home a little after two in the morning. She unlocked the door and then locked it the moment she was inside. The night had creeped her out enough to fray her nerves and she was cautious when she was nervous. Mark and Travis had joined her at the Waffle House and they'd had coffee and talked for a while. Well, Mark and she talked. Travis just nodded his head a lot and stared at the hash browns he'd ordered and then picked at for over an hour.

Don was being a tool. They all agreed on that, but no one knew what to do about it. They could talk to Sascha, but no one was sure how that would go. Sascha Wurdilec was almost as temperamental as Don, but she could normally make him behave himself.

Don had a thing for the president of the group, they all knew it. Heck almost everyone had a thing for Sascha. She was one of those annoying girls who had a brain, a sense of humor, and was good looking besides. Emily didn't exactly envy her but—

Yeah. No. That was a lie, she was jealous as hell, but she didn't let that stop her from being part of the society. Sascha's family came from some Slavic country that Emily couldn't pronounce, and she had the looks that came with it, just exotic enough to make everyone look twice.

She was also about as cool as anyone that Emily knew, and the first one to tell stories about the ghosts her family had seen over the years. Emily had met her parents once, both of them with their thick accents and quick smiles. They were too nice not to like. She had no idea what her friends' parents did for a living, but they had money. That was kind of one of the reasons that Sascha was the president. She had money and paid for all the equipment.

And Don, rude and stupid as he was, refused Sascha almost nothing.

Mark had walked Emily home and though she almost mentally begged for him to kiss her, nothing happened. The petulant part of her— and she knew it was a big part that she was trying to suppress—was stuck on the thought that he'd have kissed Sascha if he had a chance. Not that he would ever get a chance, not as long as Sascha's parents were around. They were nice people, but her dad, Ivan, was a giant of a man and very protective of his little girl.

Insecurities sucked.

"I should have kissed him."

Yeah. That was never going to happen. That was bravery on a level that might very well have been superhuman. Mark was too smart for her, too funny and way too cute.

Still, she hoped.

The house was completely quiet. Her parents were in bed and even her little brother, Zac, who liked playing his video games until sunrise whenever he could get away with it, was sound asleep, or at least in his room and quiet.

The house she'd grown up in was as familiar and comfortable as a favorite pair of sneakers. She knew every sound, every shadow, and had never in her life felt anything but secure within the walls of the two-story structure.

She looked around in the darkness and then made her way up the stairs, careful to step where the boards did not creak, where she knew her ascent would not disturb anyone. Her father was a heavy sleeper, but her mom heard almost any noise and was exactly the sort to worry. She had enough on her plate with Zac. Emily had no desire to add to her stress.

She had made it most of the way up the stairs before the front door slammed open, letting in a blast of frigid air. The door bounced off the adjacent wall and the entire heavy wooden structure rattled harshly before coming to a stop.

Emily did not scream, but her mother did. Not really a scream so much as a sharp yelp followed by a whimper.

As quickly and quietly as she could, Emily moved back down the stairs and closed the door. She made sure it was locked this time, just in case another wind came blowing the wrong way.

Her mom was snoring softly by the time she moved past her parents' bedroom.

All was calm.

All was quiet.

Still, the air seemed a little cooler than usual and she kept on her sweatshirt when she crawled under the covers.

"Thank you again for coming over," Leo said. "I didn't know who else to call."

It was the seventh or eighth time he had thanked them. Travis has lost count. He said, "No worries, Leo. Really."

Sascha said nothing. As usual she was all concentration, staring at the brown stains on the wall of the apartment's living room. She'd been standing still for a good five minutes, but Travis knew her mind was racing. He'd never seen anyone who could focus their concentration the way Sascha could. It was almost scary.

Travis was trying to use the EMT detector, but the small device seemed to be confused. The gauge needle kept running up and down the scale. Travis said, "This thing's gone nuts, Sascha."

"I'm not surprised," Sascha said. "I've never seen anything like this. And you said you tried to wash it off, Leo?"

"With every cleaner imaginable. It's like I never touched it. It just won't come clean. It won't come off my shirt either and I've washed that six times."

Travis looked around the apartment. The "blood" stains were still on the floor as well. He said, "But you didn't bring the cops in?"

"God, no. My neighbor called them apparently, but they just went into his place. I don't know what happened to him, but he's been acting weird as hell since."

"Perhaps we should talk to him," Sascha said.

"I wish you wouldn't," said Leo. "He's a grouchy old bastard and I'd just as soon he didn't know I called in the Ghostbusters."

Travis winced and he shot a glance at Sascha. She could be pretty sensitive about people taking her investigations lightly. But she was all business, too caught up in the weirdness to take note of Leo. She reached into a small case she carried to sightings and pulled out a pair of latex gloves. She snapped them on and then used a small utility knife to scrape some paint off the wall and into a plastic bag.

"Hey, I had to pay a deposit on this place," Leo said.

Sascha ignored him and looked at the small chips of paint in the bag. She already had Leo's Dracula shirt in another bag. She said, "There doesn't seem to be anything actually on the paint. The stain isn't on the wall."

Travis said, "You mean it's just hanging there?"

Sascha shook her head. "I don't know quite what to think, Travis." She turned to Leo. "I want to go and do some research, Leo. I'll call you if I learn anything. Please let me know if anything else occurs."

Again Travis wondered how Sascha could be so calm. It was blood. It was right there. He could see it and smell it. But they couldn't affect it at all. How the hell did something like that happen?

Leo said, "What about my wall? My roommate Allison refuses to set foot in here and she's probably going to move out. I can't afford this place on my own and I'm scared as hell to stay here anyway."

Travis said, "We'll do what we can, man. I'll call you."

When they were outside, Sascha said, "This is unprecedented, Travis. I've never heard of anything like this. Leo said that ghost actually grabbed him. And those stains."

Sascha was as worked up as Travis had ever seen her. Her dark eyes sparkled with intensity. She was a truly beautiful young woman, but Travis already had one unrequited crush and he wasn't starting another. After Leo had gotten in touch with him, Travis. called Sascha directly, rather than go through Don and his bullshit. He also tried to call Emily, but he kept getting her voicemail.

Sascha said, "If not for the grabbing incident, I'd have probably thought Leo's ghost a "residual," but it was actually interacting with him."

In the paranormal investigator's lexicon, a residual ghost was a spirit without intelligence or agency. Sort of a psychic echo of past, often traumatic, events. Travis had read somewhere they were the most common type of ghosts.

Travis said, "Yeah, and did you notice that there weren't any bloodstains left on Leo's skin. Just the shirt and the apartment surfaces."

Sascha said, "I did. I want to get Leo's shirt analyzed, though I suspect it may be like the wall and that the ectoplasm, or whatever the substance is, isn't actually on the shirt any more than it was on the paint."

"You don't think we might be a little out of our depth here, Sascha?"

Sascha smiled. "Perhaps. Let's dig a little more before we talk to anyone else. This could be a very important discovery, Travis. I don't want anyone stealing it from us."

Cindy had told herself she wouldn't go back to Wellman, no matter what her "vision" told her. And yet, here she was, on a bright, cold Sunday morning, rolling up Hwy 575 toward the Blue Ridge Mountains. The trees were just beginning to color. Autumn had been slow to arrive, summer hanging on like a jilted lover who hadn't quite gotten the message.

Still, it was a beautiful drive once she was clear of the snarl of traffic around Gatesville University, and she tried to focus on that, rather than her destination. Bad things had happened the last time Cindy had visited Wellman. She'd been assisting the local law enforcement with a murder investigation and she had found herself face to face with incontrovertible proof of the supernatural.

As a psychic, Cindy had always been aware of something beyond the average person's conception of reality, but she considered her abilities a heightened awareness, the fabled "sixth sense" that most human beings possessed, but couldn't tap into. Oh, her father, a noted psychic investigator, had told her some strange stories of run-ins with supernatural entities, and while she had always believed him, they were still just stories.

Not anymore. What she had seen and felt in an old house in a part of Wellman called Crawford's Hollow had forever changed the way she viewed the world. There *were* things out there in the dark.

Cindy tried to put the weird occurrence from a few nights earlier out of her head, but the psychic "bruise" remained, a gentle but insistent tug inside her head. It was much like the pull she felt when using her psychometric abilities to trace a person from an object, but it was different somehow. Like someone wanted her somewhere.

Cindy checked off the small towns as she continued north, passing Jasper, Talking Rock, and Ellijay. Finally she spotted the exit sign for Wellman and followed it to a rest stop that included two gas stations, a fireworks store, and a Waffle House. The fireworks store was out of business apparently and she pulled into its parking lot and stopped. She got out of her car and stood for a moment, eyes closed.

A cold breeze blew across her face as she slowly allowed her second sight to guide her. She felt the "tug" pulling her in the direction of downtown Wellman. She got back into her car and followed her instincts.

About ten minutes later she slowed as she saw an old, red brick church with a wide yard filled with pumpkins. Cindy had always found it amusing that many churches in the south had "pumpkin patches" as fund raisers during the Halloween season. Reminders of a pagan past still clinging to more modern religions, blurring the lines between old ways and older ways. A big sign out front read "First United Methodist Church of Wellman."

Cindy turned onto Maynard Avenue, the street running in front of the church. It wasn't noon yet, which meant services were still going on inside the church, and the parking lot was packed. Sunday in the Bible Belt. Cindy was driving a small, red "smart" car, so she was able to fit it into a small spot near the back of the lot. That worked out because the lot bordered a big cemetery and that's where she was being directed by her power.

She stepped out of her car and started toward the gravel path leading into the graveyard. Leaves skittered across the asphalt, making dry, whispering sounds as they tumbled. Cindy stopped at the boundary of the cemetery, as if, for a moment, some invisible barrier held her there. She took a deep breath and stepped into the graveyard.

Immediately, she was assaulted by a feeling of wrongness. The entire area radiated it. Cindy tried to clear her mind and let her second sight guide her. She followed a winding path through tombstones and monuments, and past a life-size statue of a robed woman.

Her talent led her to a large tombstone that was cracked right down the middle. The letters carved into the stone were old but still legible. William Avery Harrington. The name meant nothing to Cindy, but she pulled out her phone and took a picture of the stone. Or tried to. Her phone had no power. She knew she had charged it the night before.

Cindy stuck the phone back into her jacket pocket. She took a step closer to the tombstone and extended one hand to touch the rough, stone surface.

Cindy screamed as she backed away from the stone, cradling her hand as if it had been burned. In the brief instant of contact with the tombstone she felt a wave of violent emotions. Rage. Hatred. Pain.

Cindy turned from the grave and hurried back along the path. Her mind was awash with emotions that weren't hers and she thought she could hear restless spirits from all around her, screeching from their graves. She shook her head, trying to clear it. Her talent had never worked like this before.

The moment she stepped over the threshold of the cemetery, the screaming stopped as if a switch had been thrown. Cindy leaned on her car, trying to get her breathing back to normal and waiting for her knees to stop shaking. She was startled by the sudden ringing of her phone. The phone that had been without power only minutes before.

Cindy checked the screen, then took the call.

"Dad!" Cindy said. "Oh jeez, am I glad you called."

Just across the street from the Shallow Falls Apartments is the farm of William and April Harper. It's not a gigantic farm, but it's big enough. The forty acres has a large corn field and a small apple orchard. The orchard does enough business in the fall season to guarantee a successful year. People come to pick their own apples, and to buy boiled peanuts and apple butter, and fried apple pies at prices that are a little high, but competitive. The fact that April uses old family recipes for her apple pies and cakes doesn't hurt, especially since her grandmother, Elizabeth, was the champion baker at several different county fairs over her long life.

Another popular fall feature is a pumpkin patch on a section of field close to the road. The Harpers are always careful to plant a new crop just at the right time to bear results in early October, barring an early frost. Between the apples and the pumpkins, Harper Farm is a popular Halloween destination for locals and out of towners alike.

William is, in most people's estimation, far too young to be as dour as he is. They're wrong. He's not dour, he's just shy and has that sort of face. April is a beauty, and one that has caught more than one eye. She is also faithful to her husband, and the mother of three little ones who keep her too busy to ever consider a wayward thought.

The little ones, Emmet, Lydia and Billy, are just young enough to be cute without causing too much trouble. They are the exact sort of kids their parents wanted to have.

In the far south field of the farm, at the edge of the orchard, there are seventeen bodies buried deep. A long stone wall, that looks like it would be at home in New England, rests between the corn and the orchard. It is under that wall that the bodies were buried and where they eventually decomposed into so much soil.

On the southern side of that wall is where William put up his scarecrow. The form is nailed to a cross and stares out with an idiot grin, looking lazily over the corn fields.

Over the years that scarecrow has seen things. It was witness to the time that William and April got caught up in the moment and made love in the freshly tilled soil. It was present when William and his younger brother had their falling out over the land. William inherited everything, and Jeremy resented it. They came to blows and no resolution ever came of their disagreement. That old scarecrow has seen a lot over the years, and heard more of William's woes that even April has been witness to.

Though he could hardly be called a member of the family, that old scarecrow has seen plenty in his time and, if he could talk, he might even be said to have an opinion about a lot of things.

As the sun set on the day that Cindy Kane came back to Wellman, the scarecrow bore witness to other things.

Jeremy Harper came onto the property in a sad state, intoxicated and angry.

He took the time to empty his bladder on the wooden stake that held up William's scarecrow, and to spit on the burlap face of the thing as if it were, in fact, his brother.

"Fuck yourself, Billy." He hissed. "Half of this should be mine."

He glared at the scarecrow.

The scarecrow stayed exactly where it was, and the wind came along and shook its straw hair and rustled the old hat the thing wore. The hat could hardly escape as it had been nailed in place some time back.

Jeremy glared some more, practically daring the scarecrow to disagree.

When he moved past the scarecrow into the corn fields, the wind howled in impotent fury and nearly blew him off his feet.

Jeremy did not care. He had plans, you see. They were not well thought out plans, but they were plans just the same. He intended to beat his brother senseless until William agreed to share the farm. He would make his point clearly known with actions this time instead of just with words. Words weren't enough. They almost never were. Back when he and April had met, his words weren't enough to make her stay with him instead of being with his older brother, and when their father had written his will his words weren't enough to make his dad split the property. William had always planned on being a farmer and Jeremy had wanted more out of his life, but that didn't mean he didn't want something to fall back on.

Their father had left Jeremy almost fifty thousand dollars, but it hadn't lasted very long. It sure had seemed like a lot of money at the time, but he'd blown through it handily enough and when it was gone he'd looked to William, his bastard of a brother, to help him through the hard times.

William had different ideas, and April still thought William was just about perfect.

Jeremy spat at the closest stalk of corn to show his dissatisfaction. The corn didn't much seem to care, though the wind sighing through the towering stalks made a rattling noise that sounded a bit like a loud hiss.

Jeremy managed to get himself lost in the field within minutes and then started cursing his brother again for the inconvenience. After a few minutes of raging against William, his mind turned to April and he wandered around calling her name, wishing she would come find him and see the error of her ways.

Off to the south of him the wind blew and carried the sounds of people moaning and crying in pain. Thinking of how poorly his life had gone so far, Jeremy wanted to join them. He knew the sounds well enough. He'd practically grown up with them. He knew all the old legends about the people tortured and killed in the area and he'd wept at the injustice more than once, when he wasn't fantasizing about being the man who held that much power over men and women alike.

Guilt washed through him at the notion and Jeremy stumbled around, pushing angrily past the corn as his face flushed with shame. How foolish, to feel guilty about thoughts that would never manifest. Even if the chance ever came about, he'd never treat people that way!

"I couldn't do it," he assured the rustling corn. "I was raised better than that."

The corn did not answer.

The scarecrow, however, responded.

Jeremy was still protesting his innocence of deed, if not thought, when the raggedy shape burst from between the rows of corn and caught him by the throat.

The idiot grin on the old burlap face did not change at all as it lifted Jeremy from the ground and held him in the air. His feet kicked at straw legs that shouldn't have held anything near his weight, but the legs did not buckle and felt nothing.

He tried to apologize for pissing on the scarecrow, but it did not seem to care. It just smiled its vacuous smile and continued crushing his throat until Jeremy died.

His body was buried under the stone wall, where it would likely never be found.

By the time the sun rose the scarecrow was back where it had been placed before, and when William looked at it, he smiled as he always had.

The silly old shape pleased him. It was a good scarecrow and one he'd often thought reminded him of his brother before the alcohol made him into such a damned fool.

At the Harper farm life went on as it had before. Unchanged by events of the previous night. William loved his wife and April loved her husband. They both loved their children fiercely.

At the end of the day, did anything else really matter?

––––––––––

Travis woke up from a dead sleep, his heart racing and his breath coming in harsh gasps. He sat up in his lonely bed and stared at the wall, his eyes seeing Emily.

He uttered her name under his breath and looked over to the picture of the whole group gathered together for last year's Halloween event. Emily's image smiled shyly at him from the picture and made him feel a little better.

What the hell was it he'd been dreaming? He didn't know but he was pretty sure Emily was involved, and that she'd been in some kind of trouble.

That thought made him nervous.

The clock on his nightstand told him it was almost three in the morning. The real witching hour according to Don. The only reason they hadn't been out in the cemetery the other night at three a.m. was simply because no one was willing to lose that much sleep.

Still, Travis looked at the time and felt an involuntary shiver.

He couldn't remember a damned thing about the dream except Emily being in trouble and he couldn't get past that feeling from the dream even as he grew more conscious. What was wrong with him? Certainly, the things he and Sascha had seen that day had put him on edge. That was probably it.

Travis climbed out of bed and shivered at the early morning chill in the air.

He had no plans of going anywhere, of course. That very notion was as foolish as could be. He kept telling himself that too, even as he pulled on his jeans and his shoes and his thickest sweatshirt.

Just a quick look at the outside of her place, just to make sure she was okay, that was all.

Stupid notion, he knew that.

Still, he crept from the house as quietly as he could.

Still, he climbed on his old ten-speed bike and quietly pedaled his way across half of Wellman, just to make sure that Emily was okay, and tried to convince himself that he wasn't being creepy at all.

He was winded when he reached Emily's neighborhood. He didn't bike as much as he used to, but his beater Toyota had a hole in the muffler and would have woken his parents. He needed to get his own place, like Mark, but he was paying part of his tuition at Gatesville University to supplement a small scholarship.

Travis leaned his bike against a tree a couple of houses away from the Strand house and went the rest of the way on foot. He'd make less noise that way. All he needed would be to wake Emily's mom and then Emily would think he was stalking her.

The family who lived across from the Strands traveled a lot and their house was dark and pretty obviously empty just now. Travis took advantage of their absence to take cover in the shadows near a big oak in their front yard.

There was only one light showing at the Strands and that was the dim, flickering glow of a television in a window on the second floor. That was Zac's room and Travis knew that Emily's brother slept with the TV on. Other than that, the house looked quiet.

Travis leaned against the tree, trying not to think about Emily sleeping only fifty yards away. He really needed to make some kind of move. At least then he'd know that she just wasn't interested. But that could screw up their friendship and though he was interested in Emily romantically, they really were good friends. He didn't want to blow that, but he also didn't want to be that creepy guy who waited around hoping friendship would turn into something else.

A dog howled in the distance. And then another took up the call. Neither was close by, but the sound was still unsettling, there in the darkness. He shook his head at his own reaction. Given the things he'd seen in the last couple of days he had good reason for being jumpy, but just because he and Sascha had found some seriously weird stuff, it didn't mean everything had a supernatural explanation.

Nothing was happening at Emily's place. He needed to drag his sleepy ass home and go back to bed. He had both work and school later on.

Then Travis saw the shadow. Or at least, what he took for a shadow. Something dark and insubstantial appeared near the roof of the Strand House. As Travis watched, the shadowy form drifted down to hover just outside Emily's window. He felt his mouth go dry. What was he looking at?

As he watched, a second shadow-form appeared close to the first. The "front" of this one was turned more towards him. It had a face. Its face was a skull. A long, black garment, like a tattered robe from some dark religion, hid the rest of the figure, and the trailing ends of the robe seemed more transparent than the rest of the thing, as if its body faded the farther it got from the head.

Travis felt his whole body go cold as he stared at the floating things. What were they and what did they want? Then he remembered where he was. They were hanging in space outside of Emily's bedroom.

Panic made him act. Travis stepped out of the shadows and into view, still staring up at the apparitions. They noticed him instantly. One of the things turned to look directly at him. Even though its face was like a human skull, it still had eyes. Wide, lidless staring eyes. That was somehow the worst part.

For a moment, the thing just glared at Travis, and then it uttered a high-pitched, shrieking cry and hurtled toward him. Hands appeared from beneath the robe and now that it was closer, Travis could see the creature wasn't entirely a skeleton, but instead had what looked like shrunken, almost petrified skin and sinew over the bones.

Heart hammering, Travis began backing away, then turned and ran. He'd wanted to get their attention and now he had. Another piercing scream almost froze him in place, and glancing over his shoulder, he saw that the thing was right on top of him, its thin fingers, tipped with sharp, broken nails stretched out to grasp and rend.

Travis put his head down and ran harder. He felt something latch onto his hoodie, and he screamed as he lunged forward, fabric ripped and Travis stumbled, but he kept his footing and ran on.

He ran for what seemed like forever, with no idea of where he was going. He ran until his legs gave out and his chest burned with exertion.

Finally, when he was down to a staggering walk, he stopped and dared to look back again. The shrieking phantom was gone.

Travis stood with his hands on his knees, trying to get his breathing back to normal, and to let his heartbeat slow down. His legs were shaking, but then so was everything else. He looked back the way he had come and saw nothing.

Travis wanted to go home and hide in his room, but the things, whatever they were, had been looking at Emily's window. He couldn't just leave. Only one of the creatures had come after him. What had the other one done? As afraid as he was, and as much as he dreaded going back to the Strand house, he had to make sure Emily was all right.

Travis turned and began to walk back toward Emily's house.

The Thaddeus Keller Burke Estate

Thaddeus Keller Burke was not a kind man, according to most of the stories told about him. A successful businessman, a pillar of the community in Wellman, he was well respected but not well liked.

There were stories that he abused his wife and children, but they were exactly the sorts of tales that are whispered, and not spoken of in polite society. Depending on who you talk among the few remaining people who claim to have known him. Burke's family either left in the middle of the night or they were killed by him and their bodies disposed of.

Here's what is actually known for certain. In 1927 Thaddeus Burke was found dead in his home. His corpse was situated on what was allegedly his favorite recliner, still holding onto a thick book written in Latin. The name of the book was impossible to identify, as the cover had been severely burned along with Burke himself. The old manuscript was apparently handwritten and there were several illustrations, but no one has been able to identify the volume by name or describe the images held within with any semblance of accuracy.

The cause of death attributed to Thaddeus Burke was "Spontaneous Human Combustion." According to the photographs and descriptions left in the coroner's report, Thaddeus Burke was apparently reading his book, smoking one of his cigars and drinking a glass of scotch when he caught fire. There is no sign that he struggled, or that he suffered, but his body was burned so completely that when the undertakers attempted to move him his form collapsed into little more than ash. Unconfirmed rumors state that his heart, while blackened, did not burn with the rest of him. If true, there is no record of what was done with the organ after his death.

As his wife Joan, and children, Joshua and Laurette, had allegedly run away from his domineering ways, and there is no record of any other family members, the entire estate sat in probate for many years before being claimed by the county for back taxes.

Allegations that Burke was the leader of a cult began circulating a few years after his death. According to those claims, Burke, along with several others figures who were never identified, would gather together on the property he owned and perform blasphemous rites to Satan or more obscure demons.

Though there is no proof of any of these claims, more than twenty documented phone calls have been made to the Brennert County Sheriff's Department stating that several cloaked figures or "dark monks" have been spotted moving through the woods and fields around the land that Burke once owned. Some have even said that the monks were seen inside the old estate home that has been marked as a national landmark by the Brennert County Preservation Society, though no one has lived there since Burke himself passed away. That the land rests between two separate cemeteries only adds to the mystique.

Alan Fowler poured himself a drink and then reached down and rubbed the itchy spot behind Buster's left ear. The dog groaned and sighed his pleasure at the contact and his heavy tail thumped the floor several times as he pushed his head more into Alan's hand.

"You're my good boy, Buster. I love you." The tail thumped faster and then settled as Alan leaned back in his chair.

Alan didn't imbibe very often. Just three times a year. At Christmas he'd have a sip of whatever was offered when the family got together. Usually it was eggnog that had been spiked. At New Year's he'd have a sip of champagne to ring in thoughts of prosperity and joy. And then there was the anniversary of Scarlett's death.

It was the eighth anniversary, so he poured himself a snort of Jim Beam and held it in his hands for several minutes, rolling the glass back and forth, studying the way the liquid and the ice moved together, watching the light break on the single ice cube that pushed through the surface tension and caught the candle flames, sending off little sparks of reflected energy.

There was nothing he hadn't said a hundred times before, thought a million times since her death, but still he thought about her, remembered her, and mourned her loss.

Maybe they'd fought a few times. Maybe he'd had harsh words for her and she for him, but at the end of the day she was still the woman he'd loved with all of his heart, and he still missed her every single day. He tried to forgive himself the old guilt over foolish arguments. Mostly he succeeded. Mostly. But on nights like this, when he remembered finding her dead on the living room floor, he could never quite escape the idea that he could have somehow been better to her. Could have made her too short life a happier one.

That, despite the fact that he looked at her face in a hundred photos around the house and she was smiling in every picture, staged and candid alike. Eight years, and the wounds were still fresh. The memories still precious. His sister, Elaine, God love her, still got on his ass for not moving on with his life. He appreciated the attempts but did not necessarily agree with them.

Scarlett had been one of a kind and she had been taken too soon by an aneurism that filled her brain with blood until that wonderful mind of hers drowned in it.

The light from the drink broke into shards as the fresh sting of tears got into his eyes.

"Miss you, my love. Every day and all the time."

The words were whispered.

There was no one there to hear them but him, of course.

The scream that cut through the room was loud enough to make his hair follicles vibrate. He dropped the glass of whiskey and tried to catch it, failed, watched the liquor slip from the crystal and cascade down to the living room carpet before the glass itself bounced twice and then sat upright on the plush shag.

He wasn't thinking about the alcohol he'd spilled. He was thinking only of the gut-wrenching sorrow of the wailed scream.

Alan stood up from his seat and looked around, eyes wide and heart stuttering along at twice the normal speed as adrenaline pulsed through his body.

None of the bodily issues was made any easier when he saw Scarlett looking at him and reaching for him with desperate need. Scarlett was dead. He knew that. He understood it on a nearly molecular level, so seeing her staring at him and straining as if against a powerful wind to reach for him, was enough to draw a sob of agony from him.

Dead Scarlett opened her mouth and another wail of sorrow came from her. She looked to him, her eyes locking with his, and then looked back over her shoulder, fear making a hideous mask of her nearly perfect features.

Alan reached for her. He was terrified, yes, but he also couldn't hope to deny her any comfort he could offer.

Alan reached for her, and his fingers crossed through hers, burning with a horrid cold as his skin passed through the spot where her hands appeared.

A moment later she screamed again, this time the sound loud enough to shake the windows in his living room.

Buster, the dog who was his constant companion, erupted into a fit of barks and then whimpered and backed out of the room, not looking at Alan or Scarlett, but at something behind the vision of Alan's deceased wife.

There was a darkness in the air, a pressure that seemed to suck the breath from Alan. Buster turned and bolted, whimpering, as that darkness loomed closer. He could not see anything, not really, but Alan felt it.

And Scarlett saw whatever it was. Her face showed how frightened she was, even as that force behind her attacked, pulling her back toward it.

Alan let out a scream of his own as Scarlett's shape distorted, stretching like taffy and straining to get away from whatever it was that grabbed her, pulled and tore at her shape, ripping pieces of her away like so much cotton candy. Oh, how she screamed, and Alan joined her, though there was nothing he could do to protect the woman who had haunted him even when she was alive.

Alan threw himself at the darkness, and fell across the ground where it waited and feasted on his one true love.

A moment later Scarlett was gone and that hideous presence left with her.

Alan was still there, however, and he crawled across the ground, tormented by the screams of a woman eight years dead.

———————

"Why didn't you just call me?" Emily said.

Travis paused at sipping his coffee and said, "What would I have said? Hey Emily, I had a bad dream. You should probably check out your windows for weird ghosts."

They were sitting on opposite sides of a booth in a Waffle House on Hwy 41 just outside Wellman. Neither of them had classes that morning, which was good because Travis was dead on his feet. He had seen no sign of the skull-phantoms when he got back to Emily's place, but he had watched until sunup. He *had* called her a little after 7:00 and asked her to meet him at the Waffle House.

Emily said, "Yeah, you're right. I'd have probably just told you to go back to sleep. Jeez, Travis. What the hell is going on? Those things you saw sound horrible."

"They were. I was afraid I was going to have a heart attack when the one came after me."

"And the other one was just floating there, looking at me sleep. Jesus."

A shower of dry leaves fluttered against the window, making scrabbling sounds against the glass. Their waitress, a woman named Susan, who had been working there for as long as Travis could remember, stopped by and refilled their cups.

When Susan was out of earshot, Travis said, "Things have been getting weirder and weirder ever since Don's graveyard party. I haven't had a chance to tell you what Sascha and I found."

Travis related his experience at Leo and Allison's place and what he and Sascha had discovered. Emily's eyes grew wider than Travis would have thought possible as he told his story.

When Travis was finished, Emily said, "I've got something too. Not nearly as wild, but it's been bothering me since it happened."

"What is it?"

"The night we had the ceremony, when I got home, I was quiet going into the house because mom doesn't sleep well, and I'm pretty sure I locked the front door behind me. But when I started up the stairs, the door just blew open. So hard that it slammed against the wall."

"Maybe you didn't get it closed completely?" said Travis.

"Maybe, but the night had been pretty still once we left the churchyard. It wasn't really windy. And when it happened, I felt really cold, Travis. Like all my body heat had been sucked out of me. I kept thinking about what you'd said about not looking back when you leave a graveyard."

"I guess it could be connected with the skull-phantoms."

Emily smiled. "Is that what you're calling them? Skull-phantoms?"

"It seems to fit."

"Yeah, but it sounds like something from the old He-Man cartoons your dad's always watching."

"Yeah, I guess it does."

They were quiet for a moment, and then Emily said, "What are we going to do, Travis?"

Travis said, "Well, Sascha isn't going to like it, but I think it's time we talked to someone."

"You mean Charon?"

"Yeah. Her shop opens at ten. You up for a ride to Gatesville?"

"Yes. I agree we need some advice. I don't think I can go to bed knowing those things might be out there."

"You okay with driving? We can swing over to my house and get my car."

"No, I'm good. I still can't believe you rode that old bike all the way over to my neighborhood."

"Couldn't think of any other plan."

Emily said, "I haven't really said thank you, Travis, but thanks for looking out for me. That was very brave of you."

Travis waved off the compliment, but his heart lifted for the first time since seeing the Skull-phantoms. He suspected they all were going to have to be brave in the near future.

Take a left on Main Street in Wellman and after a mile or so it becomes Scufflegrit Street. From there it leaves the center of town and heads up to Mooney's Bluff, where some of the very richest houses in town can be found.

The houses have mostly been built since the early nineteen hundreds, but often they were built on land that had previously held farms, or even the occasional plantation.

This stretch of land, aside from being one of the most affluent in the area, also holds tales of two separate ghostly encounters. The first is the Wailing Widow, believed to be the specter of Amelia Crawford, who lost her husband to a mining accident and threw herself from the bluffs and into the deep ravines in the area. It was two weeks before her remains were found, and even then she was only spotted because Evander Hollis heard the widow's weeping and crying and followed the noise to where her remains lay buried in shadows.

Look far enough into the history of the area and you can find the plots where both the Crawford family and the Hollis clan had their ancestral homes. Both groups still live in the same locations today.

It is far harder to find any information on the remains of the 71st Confederate Volunteer Regiment, a group that started near Kennesaw Mountain and lost their lives in Wellman.

According to legend the group fought a brutal engagement against Tucker's Raiders, a group of Union soldiers who harassed them and used unconventional tactics to whittle them away until the last man fell.

The truth is harder to ascertain.

There are rumors that the group was led astray with promises of lost gold. Other tales claim the 71st was caught in a freak blizzard and froze to death, or that they were lost to cannon fire after a particularly brutal conflict. There are even a few tales claiming that they were slaughtered by Moon-Eyes, the alleged "little people" who haunted the area for generations.

Here is what is known: The 71st Confederate Volunteer Regiment started in Kennesaw and did, in fact, arrive in Wellman during the Civil War. The bodies of at least thirteen members of the battalion were found on what is now Scufflegrit Street. All were wasted away as if severely starved, and all carried weapons and ammunition enough for a prolonged conflict.

Doctor Thomas Ingers, a physician well known to the area and trusted as a capable surgeon, declared the men dead and filled out certificates stating as much. The only noted injuries were "apparently animal bites made after death."

There are numerous recorded claims that the "Midnight Brigade" still haunts Scufflegrit Street late at night usually only showing up between the hours of midnight and three a.m. Depending on the eyewitness the soldiers are silent and move through the night without looking at any witnesses, they are a noisy lot who "hoot and holler" as they pass by, or they come complete with a cannon that they fire at anyone getting too close. Naturally the cannonballs do no harm.

Whatever the case the 71st Confederate Volunteer Regiment has added their own unique dimension to the flavor of ghosts in the Brennert County annals.

———

The road leading down into Wellman from all routes north of the town center are a nightmare of twists and turns. Not a problem if you're in a car, but the average tractor-trailer would be wiser to avoid the backroads and stick to the interstate.

Jorge Reyes was from the area and had no fear of Scufflegrit Street. He was known to bet a few of the non-locals that he could make it through the area in twenty minutes and never touch the highway. Only fools took him up on the wager. Over the years he had met several fools. Not enough to buy a house, but surely enough to pay his rent once or twice.

It wasn't a bet that had him cutting through the shorter route that night, but his desire to finish his trip as efficiently as he could. The sun had just set and he was tired, but he was also excited about the idea of parking his rig at the back door of the All Good Grocery and going home for the night.

Three days on the road was enough. If he took the interstate, he was home in forty-five minutes. If he took the backways, he was home in twenty. No contest at all as far as he was concerned. Imelda was over eight months along in her pregnancy and he wanted to be home with her in case she decided to go into labor early like her mom had done with six kids.

He wanted to be home. At the end of the day that was what mattered most.

He didn't speed. Speeding along Scufflegrit in a trailer was like strapping a solid rocket fuel booster to your car and lighting it up. Stupid was the word. No, Jorge took his time and held no grudge against anyone that wanted to pass him on the two-lane road. Best not to have an accident and especially best not to piss off the local sheriff. He had to live here when he wasn't traveling. Carl Price was a nice enough man, but he was unforgiving when it came to speeders in big rigs.

Just past the intersection of Scufflegrit and Piedmont Road there was a bridge that narrowed enough to make him nervous anyways, so he was taking his time. He'd already saved himself almost half an hour by taking the shortcut. The men in their confederate uniforms stood directly in the road, walking without any real formation.

Jorge had time to work the brakes and honk his horn before he was in their midst. He screamed when he saw them and screamed a second time when the first of them disappeared under the front of his truck with a loud crunching noise. There was no way he could stop in time without jackknifing his rig and taking out the three cars he saw coming toward him in the opposite direction. Physics simply did not allow it.

Breaks squealed and the rig fought hard to slide, but Jorge did his job and kept the wheels going the right direction, kept the trailer from sliding out of control, despite his sweating palms and the way his blood pressure was rising like a tidal wave.

Black lines of rubber burned themselves into the asphalt and Jorge prayed to Jesus, Mary and Joseph that the men he hit somehow came out of the disaster intact. There was no hope, but he prayed just the same.

The man behind him was traveling too closely for the road conditions and bumped the back of his trailer. The damage was all on the fool's pickup truck. He could see the shattered headlight and the wrinkled hood in his rearview mirror.

None of which mattered at all as he considered the men crushed under his truck. On an average day Jorge could be counted on to curse a blue streak, but now there were no words, just the dread of death that he had caused.

He killed the engine and set the brakes in record time before scrambling down from the tractor. Despite his fears he made himself look under the front of his truck, made himself see the darkness that rested there.

There were no bodies.

Jorge fell to his knees and wept openly.

There were no bodies.

An impossible miracle. He had seen them with his own eyes, felt them under the carriage of the rig.

There were no bodies.

Don Washington sat in his bedroom and thought about the ghosts of Wellman. The dead were restless, it seemed, and he was okay with that. The entire reason for all of his hard work was to make sure that any spirits in the area woke up properly.

"What is the point of a haunted house if the ghosts don't do any haunting? How can we prove the existence of the afterlife if nothing ever manifests?"

He reached for the box of pizza on his bed and chose a slice carefully. In moments he was nibbling at the crust and getting it out of the way, the better to savor all of the toppings on the rest of the slice.

The Society's email box was rapidly filling with requests to investigate a series of alleged hauntings. He would, of course, go through the process of investigation with the others, despite the fact that he knew several of the calls were legitimate in advance.

Out in the back of the old farmhouse where he lived with his family he heard a horse neighing loudly. Hardly a surprise as they had a dozen horses, but it was later at night than he usually heard any of the animals start making noise. He might have considered going out for a look, but he knew his sister, Naomi, would be all over any sounds that did not belong. Nomi was four years younger, already in school for Animal Husbandry, and had long since volunteered herself as the protector of every animal on the farm.

Don paused his chewing for a moment and listened as, sure enough, Naomi's heavy tread went down the hallway and to the stairs. His sister was a nuisance, but she had her uses.

A new email appeared in the mailbox. Apparently there was a ghost child wandering around on Euclid Street, somewhere between eight years old and twelve. If he was right...

Don switched his attention to the map of Wellman and eyeballed the distance from the cemetery where they'd performed the ceremony to where Euclid showed up on the map. Sure enough, it was within what he was now thinking of as the Sphere of Influence. The area from the epicenter was growing every day. Not a lot, not at a gigantic rate, but it was growing. Wellman might as well go on record as the most haunted town in Georgia, maybe even in America, at the rate it was growing.

Happily, ghosts couldn't hurt a person. They could just give a good scare.

Don was content with his delusion.

He was wrong, but he was content.

For the moment.

That changed soon enough.

The ride from Wellman to Gatesville was a fairly straight shot and usually took thirty to forty-five minutes, depending on traffic. Travis and Emily arrived around ten in the morning. They had called ahead, and Charon had told them she'd be glad to talk to them. Travis hadn't given her any details. Just said there was something weird going on and they needed her advice.

The lights were on in Charon's occult bookstore, Baba Yaga's. It sat in one of the old, brick buildings that had been put up before World War II. Though parking could be hard to come by on the downtown Gatesville Square, they lucked out and found a spot near the shop. Travis scanned the overcast sky nervously as they got out of Emily's car. He didn't think the skull things would come out in daylight, but really, who the hell knew?

"How long has it been since you last talked to Charon?" Emily said.

"Six months, maybe? Been a while."

"You think she might be mad at us?"

"She didn't sound mad on the phone."

Charon had vacated her spot as the leader of the Paranormal Research group more than two years back. She'd been in her last year at Gatesville University when Don and Sascha had started there, and after leaving school she had opened her bookstore. Mark, Emily, and Travis were a year behind their other two team members, so they hadn't really gotten to spend that much time working with Charon before she'd left.

Charon's stated reason for leaving the group had been she was just too busy with the shop. Emily had told Travis she thought Charon was also tired of Sascha and Don arguing with her. Sascha could be insecure and Travis thought she might resent Charon's knowledge of the supernatural. And Don? Don resented everyone.

Travis held the door for Emily and then followed her inside. An old-fashioned door chime sounded as they entered. Travis had forgotten how well stocked the place was. Charon sold not only books, but other occult paraphernalia. Some shelves held ornaments. Crystals and statues. Strange little charms.

Dreamcatchers and small copper cymbals on strings dangled from the ceiling, along with silk scrolls, ribbons, and tapestries. And of course, there were rows and rows of books on every subject from dream research to witchcraft and demonology. Even a small section of fiction.

Charon was standing in front of the back counter, talking with a big man with a buzz cut. The man turned slightly so he could see the newcomers and just for a second his eyes were cold and a little scary.

Then the man smiled and said, "Looks like your visitors are here. I'll be on my way."

The guy turned and walked toward them without saying anything else, but he gave Travis a short nod as he passed.

"I'll see you this evening, Griffin," Charon said.

"You will," the man said, and then he was past them and moving toward the front of the store.

"Charon!" Emily said, stepping up for a hug. "Is that the boyfriend?"

"That's him."

"Impressive."

"You have no idea. Anyway, hey you two. It's been too long."

Charon was a petite woman with short, very black hair. She wore glasses with black plastic frames and a black t-shirt with a green image of Boris Karloff as Frankenstein's monster.

None of them had ever known Charon's real name. Travis got the reference of course. The Ferryman on the River Styx. Don said Charon's name was probably Karen or Sharon and she had adopted the name during her Goth phase, but Don never let not knowing what he was talking about stop him from going on about it.

"It's really good to see you too, Charon," Travis said. And it was.

"So tell me what's going on," Charon said.

"It will take some telling."

"The store's usually pretty quiet before lunchtime. Come on in the back."

Charon opened a door in the counter and led Travis and Emily though a beaded curtain into a back room which was almost as big as the front room. Like many of the old buildings on the Gatesville Square, this one was deeper than it looked. There was a desk against one wall with a computer tower and a big monitor. An old couch sat off to one side of the desk. Charon pointed toward the couch and pulled out the desk's chair.

"This is where I make most of my real money," Charon said as she sat. "Hunting down and selling rare books." She gestured around at several shelves and tables loaded with books, papers, and packing materials.

"This place is amazing," Emily said.

"I'm proud of it. Okay, we're comfortable and all alone. Tell me what's going on."

Travis figured he would start with the most recent events so he told her about the skull-phantoms. Charon listened without comment, but her dark eyes fixed him with such intensity that it made him nervous. He had expected disbelief, but Charon's gaze showed no hint of incredulity.

"This was last night?" Charon said when Travis finished relating his macabre adventures.

"Yeah, and we came right here as soon as we could. We are way out of our depth here."

"You may be out of mine too. You'd better tell me what led up to this, Travis. Go back to the beginning."

Travis started with their visit to the cemetery and what they had seen there. Emily pitched in with the details of what had happened when she got home. At some point, while Travis was explaining what he and Sascha had seen at Leo's apartment building, Charon held up her hand for him to stop.

"Jesus, guys," Charon said. "I don't know what you've stumbled into, but it's definitely above my level of knowledge. We need to talk to a friend of mine. You might as well save the rest of your story for him because he's going to want every detail."

"Is he someone who can help?" Emily said. "Even with what we saw?"

"If anyone can, he can. I'm going to give him a call and see if he can join us. I just hope he's home. He travels a lot."

Emily said, "Is this someone we'd be familiar with from paranormal circles?"

Charon shook her head. "He keeps a low profile, though sometimes he helps the police. His name is Carter Decamp."

The Wellman House is now a museum but, in its time, it has been a warehouse, a hotel, and a hospital. The tall, red brick building that sits beside the train tracks on the Wellman Town Square has seen more than its share of hauntings too.

Built sometime in the 1840s, the building was originally used as a cotton warehouse, but its owner Cab Hembry saw that hungry travelers on the trains needed a place to eat and he added a restaurant on the ground floor. Over time, a few guest accommodations were added too, and eventually the place became more inn than warehouse. Hembry's wife, known as Miss Bess, was reputedly a wonderful cook and people came from all around to eat at the Wellman House.

Sometimes visitors to the Wellman History Museum claim to see Miss Bess roaming the halls. She always wears a blue dress and an apron, and always seems to be in a great hurry to get to where the kitchens used to be.

The Wellman House has more sinister spirits though, as well. The building was commandeered by Union troops during the Civil War and turned into a hospital. Reportedly the now missing fourth floor was used for that purpose. That floor burned shortly before World War II and was never restored, though the rest of the building was saved.

The basement was supposedly also used as an operating room, and more than one visitor has accidentally taken the elevator to the bottom floor, only to have the doors open onto a scene of bloody horror, as Union doctors rush about, operating on patients without the benefit of anesthesia. Sometimes the shrieks of the wounded and dying are said to echo up from the basement.

Walter Lathem was getting tired of being an unpaid security guard. He was the president of the Wellman Historical Society after all. And yet, who else was there really? The museum had been experiencing a rash of pranks and vandalism over the last week or so. Displays had been found overturned and items from the gift shop had been scattered around and broken.

The oddest thing was, the Wellman city police hadn't been able to find any evidence that anyone had broken into the building. The doors were always found locked. Chief Braxton had promised to have prowl cars swing by more often for a while, but Walter didn't think that would help much, so he decided to see if he could catch the troublemakers in the act.

Walter was divorced and he didn't sleep much, so hanging out in the empty building wasn't that great a hardship for him. He also didn't have much of an imagination, so the stories of ghosts haunting the museum halls didn't faze him. Walter was a practical man.

Walter was on his third night of watching the museum and he was beginning to suspect the vandals knew he was there. If they had found a way to get in and out of the building, then maybe they had seen him coming in at closing time.

Walter checked his watch. Nearly midnight. He decided to make one more circuit of the building and then call it a night. Just as he rounded a corner, heading toward the lobby, he heard something clatter from the direction of the gift shop.

Walter turned and headed that way. He wasn't really worried. Walter was in his forties but he was in good shape and he was a big guy. As he walked toward the gift shop, he saw one of the snow globe models of the train station go rolling across the floor. Someone was there, all right. He got his phone from his pocket and for a moment he considered dialing 911, but he decided to have a look in the gift shop first.

Walter paused at the door and peered inside. The gift shop wasn't very large and there was nowhere for anyone to conceal themselves. But there was no one there. Maybe they had knocked the snow globe over on their way out?

Walter heard a soft bell ring. The elevator. He stepped back into the hallway where he could look toward the back of the building where the elevator was located. He could just see it. The doors were open.

That didn't make any sense. The doors should close automatically unless something was holding them open. Maybe someone was standing up against the wall out of sight? Walter began walking toward the elevator, keeping a close watch for any sudden movement.

When he reached the elevator he stepped quickly inside, hands up in case someone really was hiding there. The elevator was empty. As Walter stood there the doors slid shut and the cage lurched into motion. Walter hadn't touched any of the buttons. Maybe the thing was on the fritz.

The elevator went down one floor to the basement and stopped. When the doors opened, Walter was immediately assaulted by the sounds of screaming. Beyond the doors, several men were standing around a wooden table holding another man down on the table top. A man in some sort of antique medical smock was using an old-fashion bone saw to cut off the prone man's right arm. The left arm was already gone.

The man on the table screamed again as his arm fell to the floor and rolled into a pile of sawdust. The doctor moved to the man's right leg, and grasping it by the ankle, he began sawing just below the knee. Blood spurted and the unwilling patient flailed around, trying to get free, but the other men held him firm.

The "doctor," a gaunt man with a shock of wild hair shouted, "They all must come off! All of them!"

Walter fell back against the rear of the elevator, covering his mouth with one hand to keep from screaming himself. With his other hand he punched frantically at the buttons on the control panel. Nothing happened. The cage wouldn't move. The doors wouldn't close.

Now the man on the table had mercifully passed out. The doctor had moved to his left leg and was frantically sawing away, grunting with effort as he cut. The sound of the ragged teeth scraping on the bone was like a shrieking animal. The doctor dropped the last of the man's limbs onto the filthy floor.

Walter was trying hard to be quiet. He knew if he made a sound they would see him. And what would they do?

The doctor's head snapped around and he looked at Walter. There was something familiar about the face, but in his terror, Walter couldn't place it.

Then the doctor's lips split into a wide grin. "Another patient! Bring him men. We must stop the infection. All of them must come off. All of them!"

The men surged forward. Walter tried to fight them, but they were inhumanly strong. He kicked and struck out at the men, but they dragged him out of the elevator. Walter tried frantically to dig his heels into the floor and keep them from pulling him to the table, but his feet slipped in the blood-soaked sawdust.

The men lifted Walter onto the table and held him there. The doctor stepped up and looked down at him, still grinning that manic grin. He brandished the bone saw and then he grabbed Walter's wrist. Walter felt the teeth of the saw bite into his arm just above the biceps and he screamed and screamed and screamed.

Cindy Kane didn't wake up screaming, but she was startled out of slumber sometime after midnight. She had the same feeling she'd had the previous weekend, and if anything, it was worse this time. She sensed anguish and rage. And this time the added bonuses of fear and terrible pain. She wondered if her visit to the churchyard had made her more sensitive to whatever was going on.

Her talk with her father had helped her calm down some after her experience in Wellman. Kane had mentioned that his own psychic abilities had changed over time, and that Cindy's gifts might be evolving as well. She might be moving from psychometry as her primary ability to being a true sensitive, as he was.

Kane had also volunteered to fly down from upstate New York, but Cindy had asked him to hold off. She wanted to see if anything else happened before she got her father involved. He was still active as a psychic investigator in his own neck of the woods and she didn't want to give him something else to worry about.

Of course, now something *had* happened. Cindy lay back against the pillows, knowing she wouldn't likely be going back to sleep. She also knew that if she repeated her experiment and went outside, she would once again feel the pull toward Wellman. Everything came back to that strange town. She had seen some terrible things there, and she still didn't like to think about them. And yet, there was something fascinating about the place.

What to do then? She still didn't want to get her dad involved. On the other hand she wouldn't mind some help from a friend. She resolved to call Carter Decamp once the sun was up. Maybe he could help her sort out what was going on. She closed her eyes and tried to relax. Still, it took Cindy a long time to get back to sleep.

Decamp arrived within forty minutes of Charon's call. Charon went up to the front of the shop to let him in, leaving Travis and Emily alone.

"Sascha's really going to be pissed," Travis said. "Now we have two people involved."

Emily said, "You can't ask someone for help and then tell them how to go about it. Charon thinks this guy can help us, and right now I'll take whatever help I can get. I'm scared to death, Travis."

For a moment, Travis almost reached out to take her hand, but the moment passed. "Yeah, me too. You're right. Sascha will just have to deal with it."

Charon stepped back through the curtain accompanied by a tall, slender man with close-cropped hair and beard. He looked to be maybe forty. Too young for the retired college professor Charon said he was.

"I locked the door and put up the closed sign while I was up there," Charon said. "I have a feeling this is going to take a while. Emily, Travis, this is my friend Carter."

"Very pleased to meet you," Decamp said. He shook hands with Travis and inclined his head to Emily, almost a small bow.

Decamp seated himself in an easy chair facing the couch. Charon resumed her seat at her desk.

Decamp said, "It sounds as if you two have become involved in something quite sinister."

"It's crazy, Mr. Decamp," Emily said. "We've both been doing paranormal research for some time, but we've never run into anything like this."

Travis said, "Charon tells us you've helped the police before with cases involving the occult."

"Yes, several different departments, both national and international."

"Do you have a degree in parapsychology?"

"No, my degree is in English Literature."

Charon said, "He's kidding you. He has more than one degree."

Decamp said, "That is so. Now, I know you've already told Charon some of your experiences, but please, go back to the beginning and tell me everything you can remember, no matter how inconsequential it might seem."

The guy really did talk like a professor, Travis noted. He had a very slight Southern accent, though he spoke very quickly. Travis started the story again, going all the way back to the night in the graveyard. When he reached the part about the cracked gravestone, Decamp interrupted.

"Do you recall the name on the tombstone?"

"Yeah, it was William Avery Harrington."

"Ah," said Decamp.

"Do you know the name?" Emily said.

"Perhaps. We'll come back to that. Please continue, Travis."

Travis said, "It might be better if Emily told you what happened after she got home from the cemetery."

After Emily explained the events at her home, Decamp said, "Yes, that's a common bit of folklore in many countries. Looking back after a funeral can invite the departed to follow."

"Do you think something did follow me home?" Emily said.

"I'll want to visit your house before I can begin to draw any conclusions, Emily. Will that be possible?"

"Yes, my parents are going out of town this weekend, so that would be good. Probably better if I keep them out of this. They've never really approved of my interest in the occult."

"Excellent. Now, what happened next, Travis?"

Travis told Decamp about what he and Sascha had found at Leo's place. He mentioned the samples Sascha had taken and Decamp asked if there had been any results yet from the tests.

"I haven't heard anything so far," Travis said.

"It's unlikely there will be anything to find," said Decamp. "Ectoplasm is notoriously short lived, and usually doesn't leave traces that can be found by common methods of analysis."

Finally, Travis came to the skull-phantoms. He noted that Decamp watched him intently as he told that part of his story, but waited for Travis to finish before he spoke.

Decamp said, "They saw you? They actually recognized your presence?"

"One of them chased me down the street."

"That puts a whole different light on things," Decamp said. "The other manifestations didn't necessarily show intelligence or intent. But these creatures had a purpose and they reacted when you interfered."

Emily said, "What do you think they wanted at my house? Should I sleep there tonight?"

Decamp said, "If something malignant followed you home and these apparitions are connected to it, they'll find you wherever you go, my dear. Going home isn't any worse than going anywhere else."

"Oh God. What should I do?"

"When are your parents leaving for the weekend?"

"Not until tomorrow. They're taking my little brother with them, thank goodness."

Decamp seemed to consider that. "Here is what we'll do. You go home and act as if nothing has happened. Go to bed tonight as you normally would."

Travis said, "Wait a second, Mr. Decamp. What if those things come back tonight? We don't know what they'll do."

Decamp smiled at Travis. "Your concern for Emily is commendable, and you've show great bravery. But I don't want you hiding outside the Strand home tonight."

"I won't let her deal with this alone."

"She won't be alone, Travis. I'll be there."

Travis wasn't sure what he thought about that. On the one hand he certainly didn't have any idea what to do about the skull-phantoms, but on the other, he didn't like leaving Emily's safety to someone he'd just met.

Emily said, "Thank you, so much Mr. Decamp. I appreciate you doing this."

"Please call me Carter, Emily. We are, after all, comrades against the supernatural now."

"Okay, Carter. Do you have any theories about what's happening to us?"

Decamp said, "Nothing concrete. I need to collect some data. It is a capital mistake to theorize before the facts."

Charon said, "Carter's a big fan of Sherlock Holmes."

Decamp said, "It does seem evident that these occurrences began with your ceremony. I'll start by driving to Wellman and having a look at the gravestone."

"You said we'd come back to William Avery Harrington," said Travis.

"Yes, one of the founding fathers of the town of Wellman. Harrington was responsible for the cotton mill which was one of the main businesses in Wellman until the 1960s."

Emily said, "I thought Wellman was founded because of the marble quarry."

"It was," Decamp said. "By Samuel Wellman in 1848. But Harrington was important in the town's history as well. If memory serves, he invited several of his wealthy friends to come and live there and invest in his mill."

"You know a lot about Wellman," Travis said.

Decamp smiled. "To someone with my interests, Wellman is a place well worth studying. It seems to have a higher percentage of supernatural occurrences than other areas, as you're now learning."

"Any idea why that is?" said Travis.

"One or two. But that's topic for another time. Right now, I want to go and have a look at that graveyard. Travis, you and Emily please contact me if anything else happens. Emily, I'll be near your home tonight, but don't look for me. Just go about your business as if nothing was going on."

"I'll try," Emily said.

Charon said, "Let me grab a few things and I'll come with you, Carter."

Decamp said, "Let's all plan on talking again tomorrow."

Travis and Emily stood. Travis said, "Thanks again. We really didn't know what to do about all this."

"I often feel the same, Travis. But I'll do what I can."

They started toward the front of the store. Just before they were out of earshot, Travis heard a phone ring and then heard Decamp's voice.

"Good morning, Cindy," he said.

The First Baptist Church of Wellman has stood at the intersection of Wellman Avenue and Samuel Poole Street since before the Civil War, though the building itself has been rebuilt four times.

The first incarnation of the church was destroyed by a fire, which claimed the life of Edgar Pimbrough, the pastor, and his wife Constance. It remains a mystery to this day as to what exactly caused the fire.

The second incarnation survived until the Civil War and was leveled by cannon fire. Neither the Confederate nor the Union soldiers would take credit for the destruction and each faction blamed the other.

The third incarnation of the church lasted until a tornado took it down in 1867, two years after it had been rebuilt from the previous destruction.

The fourth incarnation lasted a good ten years and would still be standing today but it outgrew its congregation. 1878 saw the demolition of the building and the discovery of the mortal remains of Ethan Crane, a man long thought to have left the town of Wellman behind.

Ethan Crane was a staple of Wellman society dating back to his relocation in the area during the height of the Civil War. There were rumors aplenty about the man, ranging from tales of his generosity to the less fortunate, to stories of his sexual conquests. Where he came from remains a mystery. Some claim he moved into the area from Louisiana, where he practiced Gullah sorcery, and others state that he came from Texas to get away from a deep and abiding personal tragedy.

Whatever the case, paper trails lead to nothing but more rumors and gossip. What is known is that the man paid for the construction of the church that still stands today, an elaborate affair with marble floors and columns as well as enough seating for four hundred people. Crane's money had already been paid to many of the contractors and his estate handled the rest as he left no one behind to claim his considerable fortune.

Ethan Crane must have made enemies somewhere along the way. His corpse was found wrapped in a burlap sack filled with salt, and his body was remarkably well-preserved, though his eyes had been carved from his skull and his heart removed from his chest.

Despite several rumors that other mutilations took place, there is no evidence aside from a journal entry from Dr. Jeb Ephraim, who notes only the eyes and heart removed from the body.

There are stories aplenty claiming that Ethan Crane was murdered for having an affair with a married woman, but again no proof exists to validate those claims.

There are multiple accounts, however, of people having discussions with Crane while visiting the fifth incarnation of the Wellman landmark. Jonah Roswell made mention of talking to the man about investing in a textile mill for the area and being excited to possibly have a new partner. Abigail Forsythe states in her personal journal that Crane was "kind and attentive" to both her and her mother, offering condolences to both when her father passed away of a heart attack unexpectedly. Emmet Crawford states in his personal journals that he and Crane "buried the hatchet" over the rumors that Crane had acted inappropriately toward Crawford's younger sister, Fiona. Fiona Crawford wrote in her journals that Crane never once was anything but a gentleman, for the record.

There are over twenty-five different entries found in journals and diaries, each discussing a meeting with Ethan Crane at the fifth, and so far, final, First Baptist Church of Wellman.

It's interesting how many of these claims exist, because Ethan Crane was found buried in the wall of the fourth incarnation of the church. He never lived to see the church he paid for.

Several stories have been told over the years of meeting a man in "old-fashioned clothes" at the church. In all cases he is congenial. There are three separate reports of a man without eyes staggering around the church in the wee hours of the morning, flailing his arms and screaming that he will "blind the bastard" that stole his eyes.

Whatever the case, it seems that Ethan Crane does not rest easy in the afterlife.

"No, I don't know anything yet, Don, but I'm looking into it. If it's valid I'll send it along to you."

"Well, I'm excited by the possibilities." Don's voice broke up a little as static came over the phone. He came back stronger than before. "I wish you'd told me in advance, I could have come with you."

Mark Irvin shook his head. The last thing he needed was Don pish-poshing his ideas. Better to investigate on his own before sharing with the group. Still, he kept his voice as chipper as he could. "I didn't want to put you out, besides, this is going to require some climbing."

"What kind of climbing?" Don sounded dubious now, which was exactly his main reason for not inviting the vice president of the Brennert County Paranormal Society along for the ride. Don was to climbing as Godzilla was to subtle.

"Tree climbing. I'm going old school here, because bringing a twelve to eighteen-foot ladder along for the ride wouldn't be very subtle."

"Well, just you be careful."

"I got this. I used to climb every tree in my neighborhood before I started rock climbing instead."

"Yeah. No. No way in hell, I'm not built for it." Don's voice sounded subdued for a moment. Like as not it hurt the man to acknowledge a flaw. Don hated being less than the best at anything. He would never be an athlete. Not in a million years.

"I'll call you back if this ends up being exciting."

"Call me back either way, just so I know you didn't break your fool neck."

"Will do," Mark said. His eyes were on the prize as it were, the subject of his attention already looming ahead of him. He said his goodbyes and killed the call.

He walked alone down the nighttime street; his eyes focused on the old oak he was almost certain was the hanging tree mentioned in the journals of Thaddeus Crawford.

Crawford was one of the most influential people in Wellman during the Civil War, at least if his journals were to be believed. He had passages written on a nearly daily basis that ranged from simple notes to himself about what had to be done on his various properties, all the way to entries detailing the exchanges between the various "movers and shakers" as his dad liked to say. Among those entries was a reference to a hanging tree where no less than a dozen people—ex-slaves and Yankees among them—had been strung up for crimes against the people of Wellman. Seventeen was the magic number.

It was a grisly scene and one that Mark wanted to see for himself. He'd been down Poole Street all his life and he'd seen the massive old oak at the edge of the Baptist church countless times but until he read Crawford's journals, he'd never thought about the tree as sinister.

Finding the journals had been the equivalent of striking gold. The old books had been sitting in the house of his Uncle Ray for longer than anybody could guess. That they were related to the Crawfords was something the family joked about when they considered their financial state. The Crawfords were incredibly wealthy, the Irvins were not. Ray was the fourth generation to live in the place, and if he hadn't decided to knock down the wall between the kitchen and the den, he would have never moved the musty old volumes.

Knowing that Mark was into the history of the town he'd offered the books to him and Mark had jumped, not even certain what he would find when he started reading. What he found was enough information about the day-to-day life of Thaddeus Crawford to write a full biography if it struck his fancy. Each entry was dated and filled out in the tight, meticulous handwriting of his ancestor. He'd already decided that he'd donate the volumes to the Wellman Preservation Society when he was done with them, but in the meantime, he was learning about the town's history in ways that weren't usually available, with the perspective of a powerful figure in the town's past.

Crawford would hardly have passed for an enlightened man. He was intelligent, yes, but not exactly ahead of his times when it came to matters of racial equality or political correctness. He'd often heard people talk about writers and actors from bygone eras as if they were bad people. This writer was a racist. That actor never respected women. The fact was they'd lived in different times, and Mark didn't hold that against the people. The world was constantly changing. He just hoped it changed for the better.

A wide chain barrier surrounded the tree, a polite way of reminding people to keep their distance. The chain was less than two feet off the ground and stepping over it was easy.

How much did oak trees grow in one hundred and fifty years? He had no idea, but the tree he was looking at was at least twenty feet around at the base, close to sixty feet in height at a guess, and had long branches that reached far and wide before some of them fell back toward the ground. The tree was ancient. Though he was hardly an expert Mark wouldn't have been at all surprised to find out the tree had been growing for four hundred years or more. It gave off an aura of age. A quick look around showed him a small placard that stated the tree had been growing for almost five hundred years. He took a picture of the sign with his phone and then took several more of the oak itself.

The branches were nearly bare of leaves this time of year. The ground was littered with the red and brown foliage that had crisped in the autumn air and then fallen away, leaving branches that looked like long, spectral arms reaching around blindly to snatch up unwary travelers. It was easy to imagine ropes hanging down from some of those branches, supporting the weight of men and women as they struggled to gasp a breath past nooses drawn tight.

According to Crawford's journals, Arthur Cole, a town constable back in his time, had carved a slash into the tree for every person hanged there. If that was true, then verifying that this was, in fact, the hanging tree would be easy enough.

It had been a few years since Mark had gone climbing trees, but he still remembered how to do it and he was perfectly willing. He'd have been worried if the tree were on a person's property, but it was on the same land as the Baptist church, and he didn't think they'd care as long as he treated the tree with respect.

He climbed carefully, planting his feet and hauling himself up with his hands. The going was easy enough. A third of the way up the oak there was a split in the trunk. He settled himself in the crotch of the tree and then pulled out his phone again, setting up the flashlight app. It only took another minute to find what he thought might be the old slash marks made so long ago. A few more feet of climbing and his fingers were tracing the lowest of the marks. Nineteen of the cuts had been made on the tree. They were long since healed over, of course, but they were there if one took the time to look. No doubt about it, this was the tree where the unfortunate souls had been killed.

Don was going to have a cow. If one person's death could cause a ghost, what were the chances that a tree used to kill at least seventeen, no, he corrected himself, *nineteen* people would be haunted?

The answer was pretty damned good, at least according to entries in Crawford's journals. The man made a few remarks about having to investigate the site of the hangings on more than one occasion. It seemed that people claimed they'd seen hangings taking place long after the last person had been strung up in the area. At least four entries so far claimed that multiple hangings took place as much as three years after the end of the Civil War, when Crawford clearly stated that the last of the hangings occurred fully a year before the war ended. Each entry was dated, and in every case, there was nothing found by Crawford or the men he trusted to look into the matter. Rumors? Maybe, but Don had told Mark more than once that ghosts tended to show themselves and then leave little proof behind. That was why the world at large didn't take hauntings seriously.

Don Washington could be a bit of a dork. He acted like he knew everything there was to know, but part of the reason for that was simply that he damned near did. In a perfect world he'd be less arrogant, but Mark couldn't deny the man had skills.

The phone was working just fine and Mark took pictures of the slashes on the side of the old oak tree. He counted them again and smiled when the same number came up a second time. Proof that the entries were legit. Proof that this tree had a dark history.

The wind shifted and the leaves still on the tree rattled and rustled, sounds that sent a shiver through Mark's muscles. It was almost Halloween, and the season was right for a few good chills.

The rest of the group would be thrilled when he told them about the tree. Emily was always excited to hear about potential new hauntings, and Sascha would temper that excitement with caution. The last thing she wanted was for anyone to jump to conclusions. Don would probably want to run a few of his experiments to see if he could make the ghosts more active, and Travis? Well, Travis would continue to glare at Mark as if he'd done something wrong. He had no idea what he might have done to offend, and he wasn't going to second-guess the reasons. If Travis wanted to work out what was wrong between them then Mark was perfectly willing, but until then Travis was someone he could smile at and talk to, even if the guy seemed to think he was doing something wrong. Travis wasn't in charge of anything. He was just one of the gang, so to speak.

Mark sighed and scratched at the side of his head. Above him one of the branches creaked and groaned like a ship on rough waves. Mark looked up, surprised by the noise.

Above him the ropes dropped toward the ground, thick lines of hemp that held their secrets closely. There were five ropes that he could see, each weighing down the thick branch and swaying lightly in the breeze.

Each rope ended in a noose. Each noose held tightly to a neck. Four of those necks bent at angles, a sign that the bones beneath the noose had broken under the weight when the bodies dropped.

The fifth rope thrashed side to side and Mark looked on as a man clutched at that rope, trying to force his fingers between neck and noose. He could see the broken bindings around the poor bastard's wrists. He'd had his arms locked behind his back and had almost managed to escape.

Adrenaline kicked into Mark's body and he let out an involuntary squawk. The smell of sweat and human waste came to him from the bodies that hung just above him. The man struggling for air kicked his bare feet and fought hard to get free.

Mark didn't think, he reacted. In an instant he was reaching for the man, trying to help him, trying to lift his struggling form higher, the better to get the noose from around his bleeding neck.

He couldn't form words. His mouth was suddenly too dry to permit him the luxury. Instead he lifted with his knees as his arms wrapped around the man's kicking legs, and he felt the weight settle on his shoulders and across his back. His feet braced on the thick branch that held his weight with ease.

"Just try to relax. I've got you." He found his voice. It was raspy and dry, but Mark managed to talk. The man he held onto still thrashed, panicked by the noose around his neck, no doubt. Mark certainly would have been, in the same circumstances.

The man bucked, and his knee rose up high enough to smash into the side of Mark's head. All of his careful climbing and balancing went away in an instant and Mark fell from the tree, dropping to the lawn below.

He hit hard, and felt the wind knocked out of his lungs. Any thought of moving was a pipe dream. Mark gasped and tried his best to draw in a breath, to no avail. His arms ached, his legs hurt, and his chest felt like it was on fire. Still he considered himself lucky as it didn't seem he'd broken anything.

Up above him, five nooses swung in the air, and one poor wretch kicked and thrashed as his neck was crushed by his body weight. Mark tried to sit up, to reach for him, but movement seemed impossible.

He looked up, watched the poor bastard stop struggling, and finally managed to suck in a greedy breath, to take air into his lungs again.

As he watched, the swinging nooses vanished, one by one, taking their occupants with them. The tree branch still creaked in the wind, still swayed as if weighted down, but there was nothing there to see.

Mark rolled over and stared at the nighttime sky, seeing stars in the places where the clouds were missing. It looked like it might rain before the next night came around. He could check if he reached for his phone.

He did, in fact, reach for the phone with every intention of calling Don and telling him what he'd seen.

His fingers dialed the number without conscious thought, and he stared up at the sky, and the massive old oak where nearly twenty people had lost their lives.

The phone rang four times before it was answered.

"Hello?"

"Mister Crowley? Jonathan Crowley?"

"You've got me. What can I do for you?" The voice was pleasant enough, but held an edge that made Mark's skin crawl a bit.

"I don't know if you remember me. My name is Mark Irvin, you helped my grandfather, Arthur Williams, with a problem he had once, in New Jersey, near Cape May."

There was a long pause. "Oh, yes, I remember that, Mark. What can I do for you?"

"Well, I was only visiting my granddad when I met you. I'm actually in Wellman, Georgia. There's a problem here. It's, well, it's got to do with ghosts." He closed his eyes and felt the sting of tears threatening. "Thing is, I always heard ghosts can't touch you, can't hurt you."

"Don't believe everything you hear, Mark. Tell me what's going on."

So, Mark told him about the hanging tree and the ghost that he had touched before getting knocked to the ground. He spoke softly, his voice drifting and fading, coming back again and again. He spoke only of the hanging tree, oblivious to the other issues that were haunting Wellman.

"So, what do you want from me, Mark?"

"Well, I know you helped my granddad. I was hoping that maybe you could come here. Maybe you could help me before this gets out of hand."

"You want my help, Mark?" Crowley's voice was very nearly a purr.

"Yes. Please, Mister Crowley. I need your help."

"I'll be there soon, Mark." The phone connection was broken a moment later.

Mark slipped his phone into his pocket and lay back in the grass, trying to gather his thoughts. He wanted to call Don, but he hadn't, had he? No, no he had not. For some reason he'd been daydreaming about his grandfather, a man he'd last seen over a decade ago. His mother's father had died when he was only eleven. Weird how the mind works.

He sat up and pulled his phone from his pocket, looking at the pictures he'd taken. Nineteen slash marks, all long since healed and scarred over. That was the proof he needed.

He dialed Don's number and was pleasantly surprised when the man answered on the first ring.

"Hey, looks like we can add to the story about Ethan Crane and the Baptist church." Mark stood up, surprised by how much his back hurt. He was damned lucky he hadn't broken his fool neck when he fell. "Of course, I'm serious! I'll tell you about it tomorrow, but I found a tree where a lot of people got themselves hanged, and it looks like it has a history of being haunted."

He didn't wait until the next day. He told Don all about what he'd found out, about the ghosts he'd seen, and Don asked a dozen questions. It only took Don fifteen minutes to reach him.

Don was smart enough to bring his own ladder.

PART II

Wellman Police Chief Dave Braxton stood off to one side as County Medical Examiner Ronald Pang looked over the mutilated body of Walter Lathem. Braxton hadn't been thrilled about Lathem playing amateur security guard at the museum, but he hadn't expected anything like this to come of it.

One of the cleaning crew had found Lathem's body when she had come down to get some supplies shortly after arriving that morning. She'd called the cops just before quitting the job.

Braxton had seen plenty of dead bodies. This was one of the worst. Lathem's arms and legs had been amputated and none too cleanly. According to Pang, Lathem had been alive for some of it.

"Looks like he died sometime between midnight and one, Chief," Pang said. "I can probably get it closer once I've done an autopsy."

Braxton said, "Who the hell could have done something like this?"

What he didn't add was how the hell could they have gotten in? All the doors were still locked, and the outer security system was still on. Someone would have needed a code to turn that off.

Pang said, "It would have taken several people to do it. There's no sign of ligature marks, so Lathem wasn't bound in any way. Someone was holding him. Looks like finger marks in the lividity."

"Doubt we can get any decent prints from that," said Braxton.

"Unlikely, but there may be some down here somewhere. The more people involved, the better shot you have."

Braxton said, "If you're done get him bagged and tagged, I'm going back to headquarters. The cleaning lady is supposed to come by and give a statement. In the meantime, I'll have some of the uniforms give the museum another going over. Lathem was here because of vandalism. Maybe the vandals left some trace this time."

Even as he said it, Braxton didn't believe it. There hadn't been any physical evidence in any of the cases of vandalism so far. The perps might as well have been ghosts.

Carter Decamp was waiting in the parking lot of the Methodist church when Cindy arrived. Charon, Decamp's "apprentice" was with him, leaning against Decamp's BMW, drinking coffee from a paper cup. She waved when she saw Cindy. Since it was a Friday the lot wasn't anywhere near as crowded as it had been on Cindy's previous visit.

She got out of her car and felt a cold-edged wind stir her hair and nip at her woolen muffler. The sun was well up, but it seemed to give more light than heat, and that light threw deep shadows from the gravestones beyond the lot. At least she wouldn't have to go among the dead alone this time.

"I guess I should have expected you'd be involved in this, Carter," Cindy said as she approached the pair. "Do you have some sort of radar for the weird?"

She stepped up and hugged the slender man. Then she embraced Charon for a moment. She noticed Decamp had his walking stick with him. The one he didn't need for walking.

Decamp said, "Sometimes, my dear. But in this instance, you were aware of this before I was. I only learned about this new bout of strangeness in Wellman this morning."

"But you already have a better idea of what's going on, I bet."

Decamp smiled. "I have, perhaps, more information about the occurrences."

"Well, in any case, I'm really glad you're here. Both of you. Like I told you on the phone, I had a very frightening experience here. I really didn't want to come back, but I had another psychic incident last night, and I felt like I had to."

"I'm not at all surprised," said Decamp. "You've shown yourself to be very brave."

Cindy said, "I don't know about all that, but I appreciate the vote of confidence. Anyway, what do we do now?"

Decamp said, "Let's go and have a look at William Avery Harrington's grave. That seems to be where all this began."

"I'm going to need you to fill me in on what 'all this' is when we get done here," Cindy said.

"Certainly," said Decamp.

They walked to the edge of the lot and in spite of herself, Cindy hesitated at the beginning of the gravel path. She really didn't want to visit that tombstone again.

As if picking up on her thoughts, Decamp said, "You don't have to go with us, Cindy. You can wait here if you wish."

Cindy shook her head. "No, I have to do this. I think there's some sort of malignant force here, and I need to understand it."

Decamp said, "Very well, my dear. After you."

Cindy took in a deep breath, blew it out, and then stepped onto the path. Decamp and Charon came close behind her. She was immediately assaulted by that same feeling of wrongness as before, and she felt her anxiety level spike. But she kept moving along the path. Having the others there helped.

She looked around at the headstones and monuments. They seemed washed out in the cold light. When she reached the statue of the robed woman, Cindy stopped in her tracks.

The statue's face was turned in the opposite direction.

"What's wrong?" Charon said.

"That statue. I swear it was looking in the other direction the last time I was here."

Decamp said, "I'll take a closer look at it. Given your abilities, it's probably best if you don't touch it."

And that was why Cindy thought the world of Carter Decamp. Anyone else would have said the statue's moving was just her imagination, or that she was mistaken. Decamp's answer was to go and investigate. He stepped over a low iron fence and went up a slight slope to the flat area where the statue stood over two headstones.

Decamp studied the statue for a long moment. Then he moved closer to it and ran his hand around the neck and shoulders. Cindy had a terrible feeling the stone woman was going to reach out suddenly grab Decamp, but nothing happened.

"It's all one piece," Decamp said. "The head hasn't been detached and re-positioned. The inscription on the base reads 'In loving memory of Amelia Bishop,' so presumably this is her image. The name isn't familiar to me."

"Another name to look up," Charon said as Decamp rejoined them.

Cindy said, "Heck, maybe I did imagine it."

Decamp said, "Perhaps and perhaps not. I'll take a picture of the inscription." He pulled out his phone and fiddled with it for a moment. "No power."

"That happened to me the last time I was here," Cindy said. "My phone started working again as soon as I got back to the parking lot."

Decamp said, "We'll check that when we depart. Lead on, please, Cindy."

She led them the rest of the way to the headstone. Nothing had changed. The two halves of the stone still stood, even though they looked as if they should have toppled over by now.

"Do you feel anything different now that we're closer to the stone?" Decamp said.

Cindy said, "No, but I didn't last time until I touched the thing. Which I really don't want to do again."

"You don't have to," Decamp said. "I didn't ask you here for an experiment."

"I know that, Carter. I've already decided I have to try it again. I just don't have to like it."

Cindy stepped up to the stone and put out her hand. She saw that she was trembling slightly. Didn't matter. She still had to know. Cindy touched the tips of her fingers to the rough stone.

It was worse this time. So much worse. It was as if someone was screaming inside her head. Wailing in agony. She felt lines of fire on her arms and legs and she realized that she was screaming too. Her eyes snapped wide open and she saw a face superimposed over the stone. An old face, weathered and deeply lined, with deep set eyes and a cruel, downturned mouth. Then the world seemed to be spinning and Cindy slumped to her knees.

All sensation stopped. The sounds. The feelings. The churchyard was still. Cindy realized that Carter Decamp was standing beside her. He had one hand protectively on her shoulder. A slender, glittering sword was in his other hand and the blade's tip was jammed into the earth. The secret of his walking stick. Now she could see that Decamp had used the sword to etch a circle on the ground around the two of them.

"Are you all right, Cindy?" Decamp said.

"Yeah, I...I don't know what happened. What did you do?"

Decamp said, "You went into a kind of trance when you touched the stone and then you started screaming. I used my sword to separate you from whatever force was assaulting you. I blocked the signal."

"It felt like something was cutting through my arms and legs. And I saw something. Someone's face. But I didn't recognize it."

Decamp said, "Let's get you out of here. You can tell us about your vision when we're well away from this graveyard."

"Yeah," Cindy said. "I want to get the hell out of here."

Decamp helped her stand and then he and Charon each took one of Cindy's arms, and together they walked back toward the parking lot. Cindy didn't glance up as they passed the statue. She didn't have to. She could feel its cold gaze upon her.

Is there any truth to the idea that cemeteries are haunted? Well, it certainly seems so in Wellman, Georgia. One only has to look at the official documents for the Wellman Police Department and the Brennert County Sheriff's Office to make certain.

Take for example the numerous reports of vandalism that have occurred at the Wellman Cemetery, established in 1804. Since the time of the fourth headstone being settled in place, there have been reports of random acts of vandalism. Eleanor Gamble was buried in 1804, three weeks after the first body was interred, and one night after her husband, Kirk Gamble, had her body interred and her headstone placed, the grave was violated. Her headstone, a solid and elaborate piece, was broken into four parts.

Here's the interesting part. The Wellman Cemetery is only a hundred feet from the edge of the First Baptist Church of Wellman, and the caretaker's house sits just at that edge. Marcus Darby, the caretaker hired to handle the cemetery, was a devout member of the church and known for his sobriety and his piety alike. He took his work very seriously according to all reports, and when a body was meant to be buried, he worked at a feverish pace to make certain the final resting place was pristine and ready. According to all reports he could often be found working well after the sun had set to guarantee the accommodations were satisfactory.

He was also known to be a light sleeper. Several reports dating back to 1804 clearly show evidence of him stopping attempts at grave robbery and even one occasion where Darby saved the life of Emery Bucks, a man who was prematurely buried. On all occasions the events took place in the dead of night, and Darby awoke and reacted quickly enough to handle the situation to the satisfaction of local law enforcement.

The headstone of Eleanor Gamble stood four feet in height, was topped with an angel, and weighed enough that five men were required to settle it in place. The marble edifice was found by Darby bright and early the next morning, broken into five pieces. Damage included the head and shoulder of the angel at the top of the headstone being "sheared away as easily as wheat threshed by a new scythe blade."

Eleanor Gamble's body was pulled from the ground and dragged nearly a hundred and fifty feet from what was supposed to be her final resting place.

Marcus Darby slept through the destruction. According to all reports he claims to have heard nothing at all as someone or something broke the headstone.

Over at the Methodist cemetery on the other side of Wellman, someone dug up every grave interred on the Garth family plot back on October 31, 1934. Halloween. The bodies of each member of the family were pulled from the ground, literally torn out of their caskets and "thrown through the air with great violence." Several pictures of the bodies were taken by the Wellman Police Department, but could not be located by local historians. In any event the police report still exists and states clearly that every single grave was desecrated, and that the family crypt was destroyed completely, all bodies removed and the structure brought down to the point that the foundation was buried under the ruined marble structure.

As with the Wellman Cemetery, the desecration happened overnight, and in this case between the hours of midnight and three a.m. Due to a "problem with indigents camping out in the vicinity," the Wellman police routinely visited the site at seven p.m., nine p.m., midnight, three a.m. and six a.m. every day throughout the entire year, running off a total of thirteen different people during that time. The records are available for anyone who wishes to look into the matter. None of the police reported seeing anything at all unusual on All Hallows Eve until three a.m. when officer Timothy Hanlon found the disinterred corpses scattered across the whole of the cemetery.

One of the most interesting cases of "vandalism" found in the town of Wellman also takes place at the cemetery linked to the First Methodist Church of Wellman. Amelia Bishop, born April 9, 1955. and died September 21, 1978, of self-inflicted wounds.

Amelia Bishop committed suicide after alleged negligence led to the deaths of her two children, according to stories that simply cannot be verified. There's no actual death certificate on file and neither the local newspaper nor the police department reports can be found. Bishop left her two children at home when she went for a job interview. According to the stories Bishop's stepfather, William Castle, was supposed to come watch the children but was stopped when he was struck by a car on his way to her apartment. Oddly, no reports of an accident on that day can be found, either. In desperate need of a job to cover her bills, with a husband who was reported missing, but never found, Ms. Bishop left her twin children in their crib and went to her job interview. She allegedly got the job at a local grocery store, went straight home afterward and found that the pilot light on her oven had blown out while she was gone.

The pot roast she'd been planning on for dinner was never cooked, and her children died in their sleep.

According to the local tales Bishop was so distraught that she took enough sleeping pills to guarantee she never woke up. Just in case that didn't work, she slashed both wrists from palm to elbow. She was allegedly found with one child in each arm.

All romanticism aside, Amelia Bishop was buried alone. Her children were buried in a different part of town, in their father's family plot. Amelia Bishop had taken back her maiden name when she divorced, and her children's names have been left out to respect the privacy of both families.

There are rumors that say Amelia Bishop's statue cries red tears at exactly midnight, whenever the moon is full. This same reaction can be brought about by circling the statue during the witching hour and asking three times, "Amelia, why did you kill your babies?" There are several pictures of this phenomenon, but none that conclusively prove the effect was not "faked." All attempts to record the statue crying have resulted in either overexposed film footage or static instead of images on video tape or electronic media of any kind.

There are many more cases of Wellman cemeteries being desecrated, but these are the most documented circumstances.

Do the dead haunt cemeteries? At least in Wellman the answer appears to be yes.

———————

"This is fucking stupid. We're gonna get caught." Kyle Decker looked around the cemetery and shook his head. It was creepy out, and his skin crept into gooseflesh when he considered the dead people around him.

"You need to stop being a pussy." Billy Evanier was as no nonsense as always. Direct, to the point, and as insulting as he could manage. There were times, almost daily, when Kyle wondered why he hung out with Billy.

Kyle shot Billy a one finger salute, while Bobby Grayson laughed. "It'll be fun, Kyle. Wait and see."

Bobby was the center. He was almost always the center. Kyle told himself that he would stop hanging with the group and it almost worked, but sooner or later Bobby showed up and Bobby had the ability to make even the dumbest ideas sound like good ones. That was Bobby's gift. He was a smooth talker and a born politician. At fifteen Kyle was just beginning to understand how important that trait could be.

He looked around, considered the idea of calling it quits, and then decided he'd go along with what Bobby wanted. He also hated himself a little for it.

The plan had started off as a simple case of going through the big, old cemetery for some chills. Maybe telling a few ghost stories, maybe just seeing if any ghosts showed themselves, and somehow it had evolved into the current plan, which was flat out vandalism.

Kyle wasn't above a bit of shenanigans. He was okay with the idea of having harmless fun, but Billy had changed the plans somewhere along the way. What had been a case of shaving cream and toilet paper to decorate a few headstones had evolved. Billy was carrying a sledgehammer, and Kyle himself was carrying a crowbar, the better to dig a few headstones up and knock them down. He wasn't okay with that. It wasn't vandalism, it was desecration, and that was a serious offense in his book. His grandfather had told him stories about a few cases of desecration that ended with angry ghosts. Grandpa Owens was always big on tales of ghosts and the like and Kyle thought the stories were probably bullshit, but at fifteen he was exactly the right age to not be really certain if his grandfather was pulling his leg or dead serious.

The problem was that he was also exactly the right age to not want to risk losing his friends because he was a wimp. Better to go with the flow than go it alone.

So here he was, walking through the Wellman Cemetery and sweating whether or not the cops were going to be out and looking for vandals. His Grandfather Owens was also a retired policeman and he told tales aplenty of locking juveniles up and calling their parents. It had never once happened in his entire life that his mom or dad felt the need to physically punish him, but Kyle's dad was a truck driver by trade and a very large man. He'd seen his father get physical on two separate occasions, both fully justified in Kyle's eyes, and he never wanted to be on the receiving end of his dad's ire.

Bobby looked his way and winked, smiled, as if all was right with the world, and just like that his fears were eased. Surely if Bobby said it was okay, then all was well.

The sun was long gone, and they walked along the southernmost edge of the cemetery, farthest from the road. From this point the average car on Sullivan Street wouldn't even be able to see them if they were carrying tiki torches and dancing on the tops of the headstones. That was for the best, because Kyle had already managed to get himself noticed on two previous occasions by the Wellman PD and he didn't think he'd get off a third time with a warning. Both times he's been caught he'd been with Bobby, but even Bobby's luck would run out sooner or later.

The cemetery was kind of peaceful, and it was beautiful in a weird way. Kyle didn't think about that too often, but he was thinking about it now. He's read an article online that said people used to picnic in cemeteries and at the moment he could understand that notion. He could even imagine doing just that with Beth Cranston, who was sort of Goth and very cute, in a weird way.

He'd have rather been with Beth than in the cemetery with Billy and Bobby and Darren, but there it was. Darren coughed, which was about as close to talking as the kid ever got. Mostly he just smiled, nodded and went along with whatever Billy wanted to do. Currently Darren was carrying four cans of spray paint in a cloth sack. The cans tinkled together now and then, almost as if apologizing for Darren's silence.

Billy stopped in front of the headstone for Beatrice Caulfield, a woman who wrote books for little kids before she died of cancer. He knew her name because his mom used to read her books to him when he was a kid and once they had come out to visit his uncle's grave and his mom had pointed her burial site out to him. He remembered being sad for a week after that, even though his mom kept reading her stories to him.

Beatrice Caulfield was buried under a stone that had two lambs dancing on the front of it. She'd done several books with lambs in them as he recalled. He was still thinking about that when Billy broke the headstone with a well-placed swing of his hammer. Bobby laughed, and Darren snorted. Billy dropped the hammer and shook his hands, the impact hurting more than he'd expected, apparently.

Bobby didn't bother with tools. He kicked the next headstone in line, and then kicked it twice more, catching his balance after every blow, until it finally fell over, broken halfway through.

As guilty as he felt watching his friends destroy the only reminder that some people had ever lived, Kyle still buried his crowbar into the hard-packed dirt and wormed it under the edge of the stone closest to him. Once it was in place he stomped down on the bar and felt a half-mad burst of laughter creep from his mouth as the stone slid loose like an abscessed tooth from a rotting gum.

Darren sprayed SATEN RULEZ on a headstone with several names carved on it, giggling as he did the damage. To finish the picture, he added a round smiley face with horns on the forehead.

The dread that had been building in Kyle's stomach dissipated then. He'd been nearly holding his breath as they walked through the cemetery and had definitely been holding his breath when he overturned his first stone, but when he looked around and saw that no one was the wiser for what they'd done he finally exhaled and relaxed.

After that, Kyle lost himself for a while. He knew what he was doing, knew what the boys with him were doing, but he lost track of the time and his exact location as the damage continued. When he was truly cognizant again, over a dozen graves had been right and properly desecrated. Stones were dislodged, broken, or marred by paint, sometimes all of the above. There was no rhyme or reason to the devastation, and when he looked over the scene of the crime he was reminded of a tornado's path. The destruction jumped over some spots and focused on others without any form of logic.

Bobby was panting. Billy was looking at his hands, and the swelling along his palms. Darren was painting the front of a very small headstone purple, still giggling. As for Kyle, his right heel was aching and despite the chill in the late-October air he was sweating, but otherwise he seemed just fine.

Had anyone asked him why he had stopped he wouldn't have been able to say. One second he had been merrily stomping on his crowbar and the next he'd just frozen in place.

Had he heard something? Seen something? He couldn't honestly guess. Stopping had seemed the wisest choice, that was all.

"That was fun." He spoke softly, and barely believed the words came from his mouth. His mother would have wept. Despite himself, he felt a flare of shame.

What did you do, boy?

Kyle's face flushed red as he imagined his Grandfather Owens asking him that question. He could just see the man's gnarled hands settled in his lap, and he could damned near hear the man's wounded, whispery voice, scandalized by what had been done. The old man was retired police. He'd be horrified if he ever found out.

"We gotta get out of here, guys. If they find out what we did…"

Billy opened his mouth to say something, but Bobby spoke up first. Bobby said, "Yeah. We should get out of here." That was enough to shut Billy's stupid mouth.

Darren's sole response was to nod and spray a swastika on one of the headstones. He wasn't a Nazi; he just liked the swastika. Weird. Darren was just plain weird.

The wind picked up and blasted across the graveyard, scattering leaves and throwing Kyle's bangs into the air. He squinted against the sudden breeze that blew dust into his eyes.

"What was that?" Darren spoke up. Darren, who almost never had anything to say, was looking to the west, his dark eyes wide in his head, his long hair flopped across his brow. His head turned like it was on a swizzle stick.

Somewhere along the way the moon had pushed itself into the air and given just enough illumination for Kyle to feel a little better about being in a cemetery after dark. He looked in the direction that Darren was staring in and saw nothing.

Billy saw exactly the same thing. "What? You pussying out, Darren?" Say this for Billy, he lacked originality when it came to insults.

Darren didn't even bother responding. He kept staring at the field of gravestones and looking for something that no one else saw.

There was a noise, and it drew Kyle's attention. He looked for the source and found nothing but darkness. That was enough to make him freeze up. The noise came from the darkness, and that darkness was far, far blacker than the night around it.

Kyle had to look twice, because the first time the shape wasn't truly clear enough for him to see. How could it be? It was like looking at a cloud, or ground fog, blurred and ever changing but there was a shape to it.

"What the hell is that?" Darren's voice shook just a bit, and he squinted at that darkness. Bobby looked, too, frowning.

Billy scoffed. "What's what?"

Kyle did his best to ignore Billy. There was definitely a shape, but he couldn't make it out very clearly.

Whatever it was moved closer. The darkness stepped forward, and Kyle stepped back. He shook his head. Whatever the hell it was, he knew he didn't want it touching him. That certainty crawled through him.

Billy looked his way and laughed. "Geez, you really are a pussy, aren't you?"

Kyle didn't answer. He was too busy watching the shadow move closer.

Darren said, "Is it growing?"

Bobby said, "Fuck this," and did the smartest thing Kyle could think of: he turned on his heel and booked it. Kyle took the hint and started running. Darren let out a yelp and did the exact same thing, and finally even Billy got the idea that something was wrong and took off at high speed.

Billy made ten paces before some part of his brain must have kicked in. "Shit! The fucking hammer." He'd left the sledgehammer behind, and that was evidence. He didn't slow down but turned in a wide arc and headed back for the best possible way for the cops to find him.

Billy's hand just reached the handle as the darkness surged forward.

The shadow-form turned and for a moment Kyle thought he could see the hint of a face, half-submerged in the darkness. If it was a face, it was wrong, almost a person's but not right. A Halloween costume. It had to be. Someone was messing with them and they fell for it.

The masked man reached out for Billy just as the boy was pulling the hammer into his grasp. Despite himself Kyle slowed down. Billy wasn't his best friend, but he didn't like the idea of someone grabbing any of them. Besides, Billy was exactly the type that would narc them all out if he was busted alone.

Billy opened his mouth and shook his head, his eyes wide in a face suddenly pale and drawn. He was going to scream. Kyle could sense it.

But Billy didn't make a sound. He looked like he wanted to. He shook his head again, frantically, and he tried to pull his hand away from the freak in the costume, but he never made a sound, not even when the man yanked him violently closer. Billy stumbled toward the dark shape and his free hand flailed wildly, and then the darkness seemed to swallow him. It took all of two seconds and Billy vanished; a card pulled into a sleeve by a magician wouldn't disappear so well.

Then Billy screamed, a long wail of absolute terror that was shocking in its volume. Kyle stared on as the dark shape shook and then stepped forward. He saw Billy fall to the ground, his face slapping against the manicured lawn of the cemetery, bouncing off a concrete cross on the way down, his forehead bleeding freely.

Billy's expression didn't change. He stared at the closest headstone without so much as blinking.

Darren let out a sound. Kyle couldn't have made a noise if his life depended on it. He was too afraid. Maybe it was a guy in a costume but damned if it didn't look like he'd just killed Billy.

The hooded face turned toward Darren and the man held out both arms, as if to hug the boy. Kyle saw the hood's opening now, saw the rotted sepulchral remains of a face inside that hood, and let out a scream of his own. He wanted to laugh at himself for being so scared of a stupid Halloween costume, but he wasn't sure it *was* a costume. The face wasn't a Hollywood monster face. The mouth hung open and the darkness inside that gaping maw seethed with menace. Wide, unblinking eyes glared from deep sockets. The light of the moon did not seem to touch any part of the hooded form.

Worst of all, it cast no shadow. He should have seen a shadow stretching from the moon toward him, but there was nothing. Every single headstone pointed a shadow toward him, but the dark form did not.

Darren turned to run, and Kyle saw the hands of the hooded shape grab his friend's face and constrict. Those hands were too thin, barely seemed to have any flesh at all, really, but they were strong. He saw Darren's round face drawn back as the fingers clenched.

Darren never screamed. He just died. Kyle had no doubt about it, the boy was dead. He wasn't unconscious. He wasn't scared stiff and silent. He was dead. He saw the life fade from Darren as surely as if he were a candle that had been blown out by the October winds.

Darren fell backward and crashed to the ground. He did not move.

Kyle moved. He hauled ass. He was surprised by how fast he could run when he was motivated. His feet pounded hard and his arms pumped furiously. His head lowered and Kyle ran for all he was worth.

He could see Bobby up ahead of him, still running but hardly seeming to get anywhere at all as Kyle did his very best to catch him and surpass him. He thought he had a real chance of catching up, right until the spectral fingers plunged into his back. Kyle looked down and saw those very same gaunt fingers slide through his chest. They did not break skin. His shirt did not stretch to accommodate them. They merely slipped through his body and out his torso.

The cold was absolute. The sudden shift in temperatures was enough to paralyze Kyle as surely as if he'd fallen into a frozen lake.

He stared into the distance, eyes locked on Bobby's fleeing form. He wanted to scream. He wanted to rage. It wasn't fair that Bobby should get away, not when he was the one who convinced Kyle to come along.

The cold pulled at him, barbs of pain that ripped something vital away from Kyle's body. He could see those same spectral fingers withdrawing from him, submerging themselves into his chest and then vanishing.

In the distance, Bobby suddenly stopped, and shadows wrapped around the other boy.

Kyle felt a completely irrational, smug satisfaction knowing the other boy was caught too.

In the end there was no one left to take the blame for the vandalism. No one alive at least.

The skull-phantoms were hungry, and at last they feasted.

Jake Repperton was secretly pleased with his kill record. Oh, he always sounded contrite when someone mentioned the men he'd shot, but he was happy with the numbers.

It was him or them he reasoned and better them.

Repperton's Liquor Emporium was a thriving business, one of the largest stores of its kind in Brennert County. He did a thriving business, and he kept his prices fair. What he did not do, was abide thieves. When it came to shoplifters, he had the cops on speed dial, and when it came to would be robbers, the sign on the door said it all. PROTECTED BY SMITH & WESSON.

Jake had pulled his weapon exactly four times. Twice the robbers had surrendered when he showed them he wasn't afraid. Twice they'd decided to take their chances.

Jake Repperton was a marksman and a champion at quickdraw competitions. Oh, not anymore. He'd stopped competing quite a few years back, but he still practiced, and damned few people were faster, or even came close.

Had that fact caused him any troubles? No sir, it had not. The sign was clear. If someone wanted to test him, well, there was nothing he could do about that. He'd warned all four of them. Only two were smart enough to listen. He was completely within his rights to defend himself and he'd go to court to prove it if he had to. So far, no, no one had felt the need to punish him for defending what was his.

Oh, the local sheriff had made noises a few times. But the fact was, he lived and worked inside the city limits of Wellman, Georgia, and Carl Price could say what he damned well pleased, but he wasn't in charge in the town of Wellman, he was in charge outside of those limits.

Jake liked Carl well enough, but he surely did not agree with the man. His father had been a bit more right headed when it came to defending against thieves. Carl just didn't know if a few hundred dollars was enough to justify killing someone.

Truth was, Carl was a little bit too soft for Jake's tastes. Not a bad man, exactly, but not as tough as he could have been when it came to capital punishment.

Still, he was glad he was in the city limits.

Jake stopped thinking about his ability to defend himself long enough to check the driver's license of a girl who looked fourteen but was twenty-two. He smiled and took the credit card handed over, and then offered a receipt, a bag, and a thank you.

Running a business was work. He wasn't overly fond of college kids—most of them seemed too entitled to consider being responsible and far too many of them tried to rob him blind—but they helped pay the bills. They were a necessary evil.

The bell over the entrance jangled merrily as the kids left. Jake looked around the shop, checking the various security mirrors to make sure no one was hiding in a corner, or trying to sneak past him. The bell over the entrance jingled again, and Jake looked over to see two men entering the store. He put on a neutral smile and nodded a greeting.

And then froze in place, the smile still there, but feeling empty, devoid of any sensation.

He knew both of the men, of course. Dwight Tanner and Malcolm Collins. Dwight was thinner and taller, and his left eye was lazy. Malcolm was much heavier, really very muscular, and his hands had tattoos on each finger, letters that spelled out GOOD on the left hand and EVIL on the right.

Jake couldn't see the tattoos but he knew what they said. He'd had plenty of time to read the writing while he'd waited for the cops to show up, the night that he killed Malcolm.

The men moved in silence, and aimed themselves directly at the counter where Jake was standing.

Jake's hand reached to the holster he kept at the register. He grabbed for it but missed. His hand shook violently. "Ah." He meant to tell them to stop. Meant to say a lot of things really but his mouth refused to form words.

The second time he reached for the holstered pistol his fingers pushed it further back. The two dead men walked toward him, their faces lost in shadows that simply should not have existed in the well-lit room. Their eyes were hidden. Their noses cast shadows over their mouths. Their lips offered no smiles, no expressions at all, really.

Malcolm walked through a display of Budweiser complete with a cardboard standee of a scantily clad witch with a pointy black hat. His foot shifted through the cases of beer as if they weren't there. He should have tripped and fallen on his face when he hit the display, but instead he moved through without even noticing.

Like a ghost.

Jake's eyes flew wide, and his hand reached again, finding the holster.

A smile peeled his gums back from a rictus grin, and Jake pulled the .44 caliber Smith & Wesson from the holster. By God, he'd kill them again if he had to.

A laugh bubbled past his bared teeth.

Jake aimed and fired at Malcom first. The bullets went through him and shot the smiling face off the Budweiser witch, who jumped, danced, and then fell backward.

Malcolm did not move.

Jake aimed at Dwight Tanner and grouped three shots into his chest. Behind him bottles of rum exploded off the shelf in a spray of fragments.

Jake's hands weren't shaking any more. He could aim and fire in his sleep and never worry about missing. He moved back to Malcolm and prepared to squeeze the trigger. Not at all certain why the man was still standing after taking three bullets. By all rights he should have been dead again.

Dead.

Again.

The revelation came to him in a wave. He'd tried to suppress it before, but there was simply no way around the fact that both men advancing on him were dead. He'd killed them himself.

He'd defended his property from thieves, from low lives who'd threatened him with guns, never once guessing that he would be faster on the draw.

They were dead.

They'd been dead for a while now, actually. Malcom had been cremated. Twitchy, strung-out Dwight had been buried over at the Methodist cemetery. They were dead.

Dead, dead, dead.

Jake continued firing until his pistol's clip was empty. He hit his targets every time, and they did not care at all.

They just kept coming.

And then they reached for him, their hands touching his clothes, pulling him closer, as if they weren't ghosts at all.

But Jake knew better.

They were dead.

"Yes, that's him," Cindy said, pointing at a photograph in a book which rested on Decamp's desk. "That's the face I saw."

Decamp said, "William Avery Harrington. So now we know."

They were sitting in Decamp's study, Decamp behind his desk, and Cindy and Charon in two chairs in front of the massive piece of furniture. As always, Cindy marveled at the room. It took up one side of the lower floor of Decamp's Victorian era home in Marietta, and according to Decamp, had once been three rooms, but his library kept expanding.

She could believe it. Three walls of the long room were lined with bookshelves and the shelves were stuffed full of volumes. There were a couple of locked bookcases, which Cindy knew held books Decamp didn't want other people seeing. Almost all of the hundreds of books in the room dealt with the supernatural and the occult. Some of them were dangerous.

Of course, other people might consider the objects on the room's fourth wall, the one behind Decamp, more dangerous. That wall held a display of weapons. Handguns, swords, knives, and a few things Cindy couldn't identify. Once upon a time Decamp had fenced in the Olympics, and she knew he was proficient with all the weapons on the wall and many others. She had been to his house enough times to know the weapons display changed as Decamp rotated the items out of a larger collection.

Charon said, "So now that we know, how does that help us?"

Decamp said, "It gives us another piece of the puzzle."

Cindy had filled them in on what she had seen at the churchyard while Decamp had dug out a few books dealing with Wellman town history. Then Decamp had told her about his talk with some paranormal investigators who were friends of Charon's. They'd also had a weird experience at the church. And several weirder experiences since.

Unfortunately none of the information they had shared had actually formed any sort of a pattern. The only obvious thing was the likelihood that the ceremony in the graveyard had awoken something. But what it was and what it wanted remained unknown.

"What is it with Wellman, anyway?"

Decamp said, "A question Charon's friends asked as well. I'm more inclined to answer you, however. Wellman is what is known as a liminal area. A place where the walls between realities are thinner."

Cindy said, "Dad has told me about that sort of thing. Do you have any idea of why that's true of Wellman?"

"You remember the Blackbourne family, I assume."

"Good Lord, yes."

Cindy wasn't likely to forget her experiences with the Blackbournes. She had visited a house belonging to the family while helping Decamp investigate a serial killer. She had almost been possessed there by an entity she still didn't understand. The house stood in a place called Crawford's Hollow and it wasn't somewhere she ever planned on going again.

"I've told you a little about the Blackbournes then, but not all of it. The thing is, my dear, they aren't entirely human."

"What do you mean?"

"They're part of a species that predates humanity. Their ancestors once ruled what little of the world existed in an epoch long forgotten by recorded history. Most of them were banished to another dimension in those long-ago days, but over the years the few who remained have been working to bring the others back here. Over time their efforts may have weakened the veil between that other world and this one."

Cindy said, "I'm sorry, Carter, but that's nuts. I mean how could there have been a world before recorded history that no one knows about? There would be ruins or evidence of some sort, wouldn't there?"

Outside the skies had grown cloudy again and Cindy could almost feel the dimness of the day pressing against the windows. She could hear the wind in the eaves of the old house.

Charon said, "There is some evidence if you know where to look. There are legends of the old race in various cultures. Even here, the Native Americans called them the moon-eyed people."

"I remember you mentioning that before," Cindy said. "And I think I saw some things with glowing eyes when we were in Crawford's Hollow. My memory of that night is a little hazy."

Decamp said, "Some of the Blackbournes are more human than others. Some of them live in more than one dimension at the same time. Twice, in recent history they've tried to open a rift to allow the rest of their people to cross back over from the outer dark. The last attempt left them very weak and almost destroyed the old house where they had set up a sort of dimensional nexus. They've been fairly quiet since, licking their wounds and recovering their strength."

Cindy said, "Okay, okay. This is a lot to take in. So if they've weakened the fabric of reality around Wellman, it makes it easier for supernatural things to manifest there?"

"That's my theory, yes," said Decamp. "Though it's almost a chicken or egg sort of conundrum. It's possible that Wellman was always a liminal area and that's what brought the Moon-Eyes there. But they've definitely affected the dimensional barriers."

Charon said, "So we're thinking that this is allowing what? Ghosts to come through? Actual spirits of the dead?"

Decamp's phone dinged and he said, "Excuse me a moment." He picked up the device from his desk and looked at the screen. He frowned as he read a text that had come through.

"Bad news?" said Cindy.

Decamp said, "Very bad. You told us that during your vision you felt pain in your arms and legs?"

"Yes. Very sharp pain. Why?"

"The text was from one of my sources. He saw a police report from the Wellman PD. A body was found in the basement of the Wellman House Museum this morning. All of the victim's limbs had been severed."

Two in the morning and Travis was crouched at the corner of the still empty house across from the Strand place. Yeah, that Decamp guy had told him to stay home, but he just couldn't leave Emily alone with the skull-phantoms. And really, he'd been here for about four hours and he hadn't seen any sign of Decamp. Maybe the guy had changed his mind.

He also hadn't seen any sign of the creatures, whatever they were. Maybe they wouldn't be back. That would be okay with him. He really didn't want another run-in with those things.

"Try not to make any noise," a voice whispered from behind him.

Travis lurched to his feet, instinctively spinning and swinging his fists at whoever had come up behind him. A few seconds later he was lying on his back and Carter Decamp had him pinned to the ground and was covering Travis's mouth with one hand.

"I suppose I should have said try not to make any noise and don't attack me," Decamp said. "Now get up and come with me."

Decamp didn't wait for an answer. He released Travis, stood, and then disappeared around the side of the house. Travis picked himself up off the ground and followed. He found Decamp standing by the back door, which was open now. The slender man stepped inside and after Travis entered, Decamp closed the door behind them.

"Do you know the people this house belongs to?" Travis said.

"The Larsons? No. But I know they're out of town until next week."

"You broke in?"

"I didn't break anything. I'm using their living room as an observation point. I'll leave everything as I found it. It's better than lurking in the bushes as you've been doing, and I can ward this place so your skull-phantoms aren't aware of me. I couldn't do that out in the open."

"Ward? What are you talking about?"

"A ward is a barrier. A way to keep things in or out."

"You mean like magic?" Travis said.

"Something like that. And you can stop whispering. If the apparitions do return, they won't be able to hear us in here."

Travis wasn't sure if Decamp was crazy or not. He sounded really convincing, and given the things Travis had seen in the last few days, he couldn't really rule anything out. Maybe the guy actually could do what he said.

"Now," Decamp said, "If you'll join me at the window, we can continue our vigil."

"How long have you been here?"

"Since before you arrived. I invited you in now, because if the things come, I think it will be soon. Many students of the occult consider three in the morning the actual witching hour. The time when reality is at its most malleable."

Travis didn't have anything to say to that so he went to the window with Decamp. They stood far enough back not to be visible to any passersby in the darkness. Travis focused on the single window at the corner of the house. Emily's window. Was she asleep? He doubted it. He wouldn't have been able to sleep knowing those things might be coming.

Time seemed to crawl as they waited. Travis noted that Decamp seldom moved. He looked relaxed, but his attention was also glued to the roof line above Emily's window.

And then Travis saw them. Again there were two of them and they descended slowly from the darkness to hang there in the air outside the window, as if they were two fragments of the night. Travis gritted his teeth because he wanted to whimper. Especially when one of them turned its skeletal face in his direction. He hoped Decamp was right and the thing couldn't see him.

"Skull-phantoms is an excellent name for the apparitions," Decamp said.

"But what are they? And what do they want with Emily?"

"I'm afraid I don't know, Travis. I haven't encountered anything like them. You said one of them chased you last night. Presumably the other one remained and it didn't hurt Emily. Perhaps they are merely keeping track of her."

"Why would they do that?"

"I hesitate to speculate, but it may have something to do with the perceived "invitation" of Emily looking back as she left the churchyard. She may have inadvertently become a conduit of sorts."

"You mean they need her for something?" He didn't like the sound of that at all.

"As I said, I'm just not sure." Decamp turned from the window and picked up a walking stick that had been leaning against a wall near the window. He started toward the door.

Travis said, "Wait, are you going out there?"

"Yes, I think it's time I had a closer look at these creatures. Now listen to me Travis. This time I want you to stay put. If they come after me, I'll deal with them."

"I feel kind of lame letting you go out there alone."

Decamp smiled. "You've already shown yourself to be a brave young man. You've nothing to prove. Besides, should something happen to me, you'll need to see that Emily is safe."

Travis nodded. Decamp was right. He knew that. But he didn't have to like it.

Carter Decamp was glad to feel the night air as he stepped out of the Larson house. He was glad Travis had remained behind. He couldn't watch after the boy and give his full attention to the creatures.

He hadn't crossed to the front of the Larsons' yard before the things became aware of him. One of them turned toward him and regarded him with wide, staring eyes. He noted that the head and upper torso appeared quite solid, while the figure became less distinct as it tapered away toward the lower part of its body, which was sheathed in a robe or shroud of some dark material. If it was a ghost, it wasn't like any he had encountered before.

The thing shrieked, just as Travis had described, in a bone chilling, high-pitched voice, and then it twisted in the air and flew toward Decamp with hands outstretched.

Decamp twisted the handle of the walking stick and withdrew the sword inside. Its silver-edged blade shone in the glare from the streetlight. Decamp pointed the weapon at the skull-phantom.

The creature's desiccated lips drew back, revealing sharp incisors, and it wailed again, but it stopped its forward rush and turned to hover in the air about six feet from the tip of the blade. Its eyes burned with sheer malevolence, but it didn't try to come closer.

Decamp took a step forward and the apparition drifted backwards. It didn't want to come into contact with the sword. Did it recognize the weapon's power instinctively or was there a deeper understanding here?

Decamp realized that he could no longer see the second skull-phantom even as he felt the hairs at the nape of his neck stir. He went forward in a diving roll just as he felt something tear the back of his coat, and fiery pain danced across his neck. He'd gotten careless and the second creature had outflanked him.

The first skull-phantom, seeking to take advantage of Decamp being off balance, swept through the air toward him. Decamp completed his forward roll, coming right back to his feet and sprang forward in a fencer's crouch. This time the creature couldn't change direction quickly enough and it was impaled on the sword. Intense cold flowed down the blade and into Decamp's arm. It was so shockingly painful that he lost his hold on the weapon.

But the skull-phantom fared worse. With another horrendous screech, it exploded into vapor, and the sword clattered to the ground. Decamp was already in motion, spinning to face the second creature. It hovered just out of reach, glaring at him. Decamp's hand slipped into his coat pocket and closed around some powder he had secreted there.

But he didn't get a chance to use the dust for its intended purpose. The second skull-phantom shot straight upwards and lost itself in the dark. Decamp walked over the sword and picked it up. The weapon was unharmed and the unnatural cold had left it.

The back of his neck ached abominably and when he put his hand there, his fingers came away wet with blood. Whatever the things were, they were solid enough to kill him, and solid enough to be killed, or destroyed.

If the stories are true, Michael Lanier killed his entire family at the end of World War One. He came home at the end of the "war to end all wars" with a serious case of what these days would be called Post Traumatic Stress Disorder and did his best to settle back into the life he'd had before the war, but failed to acclimate into that existence.

According to the few written reports to be found, Lanier, a doctor and amateur stockbroker, managed to handle his patients well enough, but there are tales of his drinking, and stories of the abuse he heaped on wife, Lee-Anne and his two children, Eli and Rose. As is often the case in smaller areas, the stories were known well enough, but no one seemed interested in interfering. There are exactly two files to be found with the Wellman Police Department. Both claim that there was no sign of abuse found when the police were called in to investigate. The identity of the neighbor who suggested the police visit remains a mystery.

Lanier might well have abused his family. He might also simply have been a man who couldn't handle his drink very well. The truth may never be known. In any event, the family fortune looked to be growing nicely until the stock market crashed and all of Lanier's careful investments took out the man's life savings and cost him everything he had earned.

Though there is no hard evidence to be found, the stories written down in various journals and diaries accumulated by local historian Alexander Cummings claim that Michael Lanier took the news poorly. According to local lore Lanier killed his family and then himself, after hiding all of the family's valuables. His wife's jewelry, the gold coins he'd collected, even the family bible, were all gathered together and buried somewhere on the property that would be seized by the banks shortly after the family's demise.

The house that Lanier owned is long gone. His family was buried on a plot of land adjoining one of the local churches, but the exact location is being left out at the surviving family's request. Almost twenty-five years after the Lanier's died, the land was used to build a new subdivision. Since then, two of the houses in the Evergreen Creek neighborhood have had trouble keeping occupants, and there are often reports of cold spots and unexplained power outages in the whole area.

The house at 227 Evergreen Terrace has been hastily vacated on no less than nine different occasions. The people who move in might want to stay in the ranch style home, but the screams of two children and one woman come around far too often to make sleep comfortable. The police records show at least seventeen different occasions where either the occupants of the house, or nearby neighbors have reported the sounds of extreme violence coming from the house. In each and every case the cause of the disturbances has remained a mystery.

The situation at the other house, 243 Evergreen Terrace, is a little different. No screams are ever heard, but on eleven documented occasions the owners have called to report the sounds of someone rustling round in the backyard or side yard, only to have the police find no one on the premises. On eight occasions, however, the investigations have found holes torn in the lawn and evidence that someone was digging with a shovel, searching, perhaps, for lost family treasures.

It is possible that a neighbor thinks they're onto something and doesn't want to share, but not likely. You see, the grass and garden are never disturbed by footprints, and while there are holes appearing and signs that a shovel has been used, there is never any dirt to be found near those freshly dug holes.

Is Michael Lanier still murdering his family? Does his restless spirit still try to locate the family treasures he buried to protect from greedy hands? We may never truly know.

The town of Wellman didn't have its own morgue. Jonathan Crowley had to visit the Brennert County Morgue to look at the bodies. He did not request a visitor's pass, but instead found his own way in when no one was looking.

It wasn't all that difficult at eight in the evening. The attendant was busy in the office, filling out paperwork, and rocking out to some screaming herd of monkeys pretending to be a heavy metal band. For the life of him, he'd never understand why anyone wanted to listen to a band that simply could not pronounce words, but instead gargled them around a microphone.

The bodies of four teenage boys had been found in one of the local cemeteries. All four were dead, though only two of them showed any noticeable signs of trauma. Crowley wanted to look the bodies over himself. He tended to look for signs that the average coroner was likely to miss.

The bodies were all properly tagged, and separating them from the rest was easy enough. They were dead, and in each case the autopsies had already taken place. Much as he tried to tell himself he didn't care, seeing four dead kids still pressed at him. That was four families with lost children. He had been down that road before.

Sometimes, much as he tried to avoid them, the ghosts of his past liked to sneak in and pay visits. Not literally, of course. That would go poorly.

The corpse of a boy named Robert had no sign of trauma aside from the postmortem examination and the resulting injuries. The cause of death had not been decided. The same was true of the rest of the boys.

Four dead boys found in a cemetery, close to Halloween, with no obvious cause of death. Crowley wished he could be surprised. It was all too common, really. He might have to see if he could find a Ouija board or any other form of invitation in the area, though like as not it was vandalism that triggered the attack. Judging by the blisters on the hands of one of the teens someone had been using a hammer or similar tool to cause damage and the medical examiner had noted the spray paint residue on another in his report.

He left the morgue the same way he came in, with no one the wiser for his visit. The autumn air was brisk, and refreshing, though he could feel the pressure rising and expected rain in the area shortly. He moved away from the government buildings and into the town proper. Wellman was a quaint place that reeked of the supernatural. He'd been there before, he was almost certain of it, but he couldn't say just when. Like so many small towns, it had a history he was unaware of, and the odds were good that history was steeped in bloodshed and invitations to darker things.

Because he was already invited, Crowley walked the streets without his usual quiet. He dressed casually enough, gray suit, a dress shirt, and an overcoat. He even wore a fedora, because the rain would be coming soon enough, and he hated getting water on his rimless glasses.

He had a meeting planned. His prey did not know that, but the very thought of it brought a smile to his face. "Somebody's been very naughty. We're going to have a chat."

He had the address in his pocket, courtesy of Mark Irvin. The Irvin kid was all right, if a bit on the chatty side. They'd had a very pleasant meeting at lunchtime, and he'd had some decent food at a local diner, where he'd seen his first dose of a clan called the Blackbournes. They might prove to be a problem if the girl, Jolene, was any example of their abilities. She definitely caught Mark's attention, and that of most of the men in the diner.

All the better if the distraction helped Mark forget about their lunch. He'd grilled the boy as politely as he could, and then blocked the young man's memories of their time together. He'd remember that they were together, but he wouldn't recall the details. That was for the best, as the kid might want to warn his prey, otherwise. Where was the fun in that?

Several college age kids were walking along the sidewalk ahead of him, and Crowley allowed himself a smile. Mostly they had the world ahead of them. Mostly they were the future of that same world. He rather missed the times when he was an instructor of young minds. They had been good times. These days the world seemed determined to end itself, and kept him far too busy for that sort of thing.

Maybe he'd quit again. Stranger things had happened, and now and then he liked to remind himself that there was a world beyond the roads he traveled.

His phone vibrated in his pocket. Amelia Dunlow wanted to talk.

Despite himself, he answered. "How're things, Amelia?"

"It's good to hear your voice, Jonathan."

"Likewise. I'm on a case. What can I do for you?"

"You're always on a case, Jonathan. When was the last time you were home?"

"It's been a while." Okay, it had been a few months if he was being truthful.

"You should come up here and visit."

"Mike might not like that." Her live-in boyfriend was the jealous type. Amelia was an interesting case. Unfortunately she had her eyes on Crowley as some sort of paramour and he couldn't see that happening. He was done with relationships. They caused an endless array of complications.

"Mike would hate it, yeah, but it's not his call, Jonathan."

"Amelia, I'll think about it." And there it was. He'd probably be visiting again in the near future. He had to make sure her abilities were being contained properly in any event. In the distant past her father had trapped a demon and forced it into his daughter's flesh to save her from dying. He had chosen a succubus to coexist within her body. The end result was simply that Amelia was immediately every man's fantasy made real. She seldom enjoyed that fact and had long since learned to mute the power, but Crowley still had to check on her from time to time.

Also, she had a demon trapped inside of her. It was a demon. It needed to be kept in check as well.

Up ahead a man who matched the description he'd been given was heading for the address written on his scrap of paper. "Amelia. I have to go. I have a target in my sites."

"Be careful, Jonathan."

"I always am." He killed the call and put his phone away. The man walking up to the address cleared his throat noisily and fumbled for his keys. Crowley smiled and moved closer.

There was a harsh, cold wind blowing, and leaves whispered and hissed a path down the lonely street outside of his efficiency apartment. It wasn't much, but it was home.

"Don Washington?" The voice came from behind him, and Don turned fast enough to send a hot flare through the muscles in his neck. He was not a man who liked strangers sneaking up on him. In his experience that often led to sorrow.

The man facing him was lean, wore glasses, and sported an expensive suit. He had one of those faces. He could have been anywhere between thirty and fifty and Don wouldn't have been surprised. He also stared hard in Don's eyes and that made him just a touch nervous. He pushed the anxiety back and forced himself to face the stranger head on.

"Yes? What can I do for you?"

He was an average man, with brown hair, brown eyes behind his eyeglasses and an unremarkable face, but oh, he had a terrifying smile. It promised pain and so much worse.

"You can tell me what rituals you used for waking the dead in this town." The man stepped closer, and Don backpedaled as best he could to maintain their distance. He did not like people getting into his personal space. Never had and never would, but the man seemed absolutely determined. It was making him nervous.

"I'm sure I don't know what you're talking about."

"Oh, I'm sure you do." That smile grew even broader on the lean face. "I'm banking on it. My sources tell me you've performed at least a couple of different rituals designed to stir the waters as it were. You've been a very naughty boy."

"Who did you say you were, again?" Don didn't like the man at all. He could tell they weren't going to be friends. The lean man was too pushy, and a little on the scary side.

"I didn't. Not yet. Before we get all cozy with the names, you need to tell me what you've been up to."

"I...I don't need to tell you anything at all." He'd not be bullied, certainly not by the sort of bastard that felt the need to get in his face. Don jabbed a finger at the man's chest and was surprised that he missed his target. "I don't know who you are, and I don't much like your attitude."

"I don't much care what you like or don't like, Mister Washington. You've been bad. I'm here to fix your mistakes and that's going to go a lot easier if you tell me what rituals you were performing when you decided to shove aside the veil between the worlds."

Don laughed nervously. It wasn't at all funny and he didn't want to laugh, but it happened all the same. "You need to go away now." He cleared his throat. "Don't think I won't call the police, because I will."

"And tell them what? That I asked you a question?"

"I'm sure I can find something to say to them."

That smile again, dark, and deadly looking. "Don't make me cranky, Mister Washington."

"I said you need to leave!" He reached for his phone. He would call the cops, by God. The days of being intimidated by strangers were long in his past.

It happened fast. The phone was plucked from his hand and the next thing he knew the stranger was grabbing the front of his jacket and lifting Don off the ground as if he were a toddler.

"You're as stupid as you look, boy."

Don let out a yelp and closed his eyes, as if not seeing the man might make him go away. No such luck. He was still there and still talking.

"What incantations did you use? DuMont's summoning? The Rendering? What pathetic spells did you find on the Internet?" He shook Don, rattled his head back and forth as Don kicked and wailed. "Answer me!"

Don told him the truth. "All of them! Every single spell I could find!" Despite himself the fear came on like a tidal wave, and Don started to cry, blinking furiously, humiliated by the bully yanking him around like a rag doll. "I looked and I found, and I used them! All of them I came across!"

"Why the hell would you do that?" The man's voice hissed, and he pushed Don away from him and up against the door to his apartment. "How stupid are you?"

"People have to know! They have to know that ghosts are real!" He blubbered the words, but he meant them. How long did the ignorant have to remain ignorant? He would prove to everyone that ghosts dwelled among the living, they would be warned.

"Let's warn about the dangers of radiation by detonating a few atom bombs." The voice was cold, but furious. "I'm going to try to fix this, Donnie Boy."

He could smell the man's breath, feel it against his face, as close as a lover ready to kiss him. Don cringed, squeezed his eyes closed, and prayed for the man to leave him alone, but there was no answer to his prayers. Instead, he heard that icy voice again. "I'm counting, Donnie. I'm counting every single death. Each and every person that dies from this is on you, do you understand me? Every. Last. One. And if the number goes high enough, I'm coming back for you. I'll take them all out on you and your stupid little games. Every single death will be accounted for before this is said and done."

The silence was overwhelming for all of three seconds, and then the rain started, a light drizzle that quickly became a heavy downpour, complete with nearby lightning and a blast of thunder that nearly had Don crawling under his locked front door.

He opened his eyes and the stranger was gone. Rain whipped across him, carried under the overhang by the wind. Don fumbled his keys from his pocket and unlocked his door. His left foot kicked across his phone and he picked it up without thinking about the situation.

The stranger was gone and he was unharmed. It was enough for now. It was all he had.

He didn't cry any more, but he wanted to. No, he'd never give the bastard that satisfaction.

The rain came down in heavy sheets, and Lou laughed as he dragged Lexi behind him, leading her through the downpour that had soaked them both and covered the lenses of her glasses to the point where she could barely see.

"Come on, Velma!"

She chuckled good naturedly at the old joke, having had a few occasions where she dropped her glasses and needed him to find them for her. "Bite me, Scooby!"

They reached the porch of the house on Evergreen Terrace and Lou dug in his jeans for the keys as lightning turned the skies white for a moment and thunder roared across the heavens.

Lexi shivered as he fought with the door's stubborn lock. The rain was definitely bringing the cold with it. He could see his breath as he forced the door open and held it for his wife. Four years together, two years married, and she still made him smile every day. He took her hand and helped her across the threshold and into their home.

"How did it get so chilly, so fast?" She squinted as she pulled her glasses from her face and groped for the box of tissues on the table nearest the door.

"I guess autumn is properly here," Lou smiled as she wiped at the lenses with more patience than he ever had. He couldn't hope to know what it was like being so blind without glasses, but he found it endearing on his wife. He found almost everything about her endearing.

"Well, it could wait until the rain is done." She put her glasses on as she spoke, and smiled at her restored sight. "There."

"All better?"

"Well, maybe not but at least I can see." She shivered again. The cold was almost ludicrous. The temperature felt like it had dropped thirty degrees since the rain started, and to make matters worse, the lights were flickering.

"We better get some candles. I think we're gonna lose power."

"Again? This is getting stupid now."

"I called the power company. You were here when the guy came over. All the wires and connections are fine."

"I don't agree with your definition, Lou." She laughed as she said it, and walked over to the drawer where they kept their candles. "I still think we need to invest in a lantern or two."

"How very *Little House on the Prairie* of you."

"Laura Ingalls Wilder rocked my formative years."

"She's good enough for you, then she's good enough for me, but I still prefer a good vampire story."

"Werewolves are cooler."

"You're still stuck on the werewolf from *Twilight*. You gotta let that go." Lou dug in the basket near the door, looking for their stash of lighters. Neither of them smoked, but lighters were always handy.

"What can I say? I dig a man with a hairy chest."

"Then I am in good shape."

She chuckled

They worked together to light two candles, just in case.

"Well, if the lights go out we still have Jack O'Lanterns we can use, too."

"Nope." Lexi shook her head. "Not until Halloween. They haven't even been carved yet."

"Slacker."

"You haven't even bought the candy yet."

"I bought it."

"I meant to replace the bag you ate."

"You have to clarify these things, honey."

When she didn't answer him, Lou turned to face Lexi. She was staring right past him, looking to his left just a few degrees, her mouth hanging open.

Had anyone ever asked him if he believed in ghosts, Lou would have shaken his head and tried to stifle a laugh. Aliens? With countless untold planets he could get behind that notion, but the restless dead were just a silly notion in his opinion. We lived, we died, and that was the whole story.

Seeing the man behind him, he would have changed his mind. The man was translucent, and he was dressed in clothes from the wrong era. He cast a long shadow in the room, but that shadow fell in the wrong direction, and there were pools of darkness where his eyes should have been.

"Who are you?" Lou asked the question as he moved between the stranger and his wife. He noticed that his breath now steamed the air.

The shadow covered man spoke, judging by his expression he yelled, but there were no sounds to hear.

Lexi moved up and put her hand on Lou's arm.

The stranger took two steps closer, infuriated by Lou, or Lexi, or God alone knew what. He looked ready to attack, and Lou tensed up, waiting to defend against whatever he did.

The shape came from nowhere. One moment the strangest thing in the room was the angry ghost and the next a darkness formed behind that spectral shape and from that darkness a hooded shadow lunged forward clutching at the ghost with desiccated hands.

The ghost screamed and whatever had kept it silent was gone. Lou heard the shriek of agony as clearly as he had ever heard any sound in his life. The ghost was gone before that wail was finished. Whatever the shape was it took the ghost.

Lexi screamed.

Lou screamed.

The hooded form did not scream. In absolute silence it looked toward Lou and then attacked.

Spectral hands reached into Lou's chest and pulled at whatever they captured. Lou screamed again as that something was torn free of his body and shoved into the mouth hidden in the hood's shadowy depths.

Lou was right about one thing. For him at least, there was no afterlife.

Outside the house on Evergreen Terrace the rain continued to fall, and occasionally thunder and lightning made their presence known. Inside the house all was as silent as a tomb. For the moment at least, there was nothing left to make a sound.

Emily watched as her parents and brother drove away. She felt a slight pang, thinking that her time as part of the central family was drawing short. Once school was over and she had decided what to do with the next part of her life, she would be moving out, and that would truly be the end of her childhood.

When the car was out of sight, Travis and Decamp appeared from across the street. Both of them looked tired.

"Good morning, Emily," Decamp said. He said it as if he were just arriving for breakfast, and hadn't spent the night guarding her from supernatural horrors.

Travis wasn't as chipper. He just gave her a wan smile and a mumbled "Good morning" as he stepped up onto the porch. On an impulse, Emily gave him a quick hug. She had learned in the last few days just how brave Travis was. She suddenly wondered if Mark would be so brave. Where the hell did that come from?

"You guys come inside," Emily said. "I've got coffee ready."

"I could sure use some," Travis said. She noticed he was blushing slightly. He could be so shy sometimes.

As the two men stepped into the house, Emily saw there was blood on the back of Decamp's jacket. She said, "Carter, you're hurt."

"Superficial, I assure you, my dear. Still, if you'll point me toward a bathroom I'll clean up a bit."

"Of course. Down the hall there and to the left. There's a first aid kit under the sink if you need it."

Decamp nodded and left her and Travis in the foyer.

Travis said, "He killed one of the things, Emily. There's a sword inside that walking stick, and he used it to kill one of the skull-phantoms. The other one took off."

She said, "I heard them shrieking last night, but I did what Carter said and stayed away from the windows."

"I'm glad you did. I'm glad you didn't see them. I wish I hadn't."

"You said one of them got away. That means it could come back. And now I'll be here by myself. Jesus, Travis. I can't take much more of this."

Travis said, "We'll think of something. Decamp destroyed one of them somehow. That means they can be stopped. And I already told you, you're not alone. I'll sleep down here on the couch every night while your mom and dad are gone if you want me to."

"You would, wouldn't you?"

"Yeah, I…"

Decamp chose that moment to return. His expression seemed grimmer than before. "I'm afraid I ruined one of your towels. Blood stains can be difficult to remove."

"I'll throw it away. Mom's always buying towels. She'll never notice. Are you okay, Carter?"

"I'm fine, thank you. But after I cleaned my wounds I checked my voicemail and texts. Much occurred overnight while Travis and I were at our vigil. None of it good."

"What happened?" said Travis.

"Let's sit down and have some coffee," Decamp said. "I have some things I need to tell you two."

That didn't sound good. Emily led the way to the kitchen, where she got three mugs and put them on the table. She and Travis both stirred cream and sugar into their coffee. Decamp took his black.

"During the night, there were several as yet unexplained deaths," Decamp said, without preamble. "The owner of a large liquor store was found dead in his business. Two other people were found in their home. Most disturbing were the bodies of four teenagers found in the Wellman cemetery."

"Oh my God," Emily said. "This all happened last night?"

"I'm afraid so."

Travis said, "What killed them?"

"That's the most disturbing part. Two of the boys in the cemetery had sustained some injuries, but according to preliminary reports, there were no signs of violence on the other two. I'm still waiting for my sources to supply me with more information. It may not all be connected to our current situation, but I feel certain most of it is."

"Yeah, the cemetery thing sure sounds like it," Travis said.

Decamp said, "There may be more. There was another killing two nights ago at the Wellman House Museum, and I'm sure it was part of this. I need to get home and talk to some of my other sources."

Emily could feel her anxiety level climbing. She said, "You keep talking about sources. Do you have like, spies, working for you?"

Decamp said, "Over the years I've developed a network of people who investigate the same things I do. They keep me informed of odd occurrences. Some are acquaintances and some are friends. Some I've had little contact with other than the internet."

Travis said, "Carter, are we responsible for this? For all these deaths?"

Decamp was quiet for a moment. Then he said, "From what you've told me, your friend Don performed the actual ceremony."

"Yeah, but we were there. We went along with it."

"I'm not a priest, Travis. I can't offer you absolution. You'll have to decide for yourselves how culpable you are."

"Jesus," Emily said.

Decamp said, "For my own part, I need to take a more active role in this situation. Events are spiraling out of control, and I think more lives are at stake. But before I go, I'm going to ward this house against supernatural entities. I should be able to keep the skull-phantoms from entering."

"But you're not sure?" Travis said.

"Not entirely, which makes it more important that I track down whatever is causing this. In the meantime, I suggest you consult with your fellow paranormal investigators. All of this centers around the five of you."

Travis said, "If you can keep things out of the house, why didn't you do it last night?"

"Do you two want Emily's parents to know what's going on?"

"Okay, no," said Emily.

"That's why I waited. And I was here from sundown until sunup to make sure nothing happened to Emily."

Travis said, "Yeah, you were. Sorry, Carter. I didn't mean to imply you weren't doing all you could. I guess I'm just tired."

"Completely understandable. Now, let me see what I can do here."

"There they go," Austen Oden said. "We should have about an hour before they come back around."

Candace (never Candy) Bowman, rose slowly from where she'd been hiding behind a marble obelisk, and watched the retreating taillights of a Wellman police cruiser as the car left the grounds of the Methodist churchyard. She said, "Plenty of time to spend with Amelia."

The police had been stepping up the patrols lately, because of a lot of incidents of vandalism in the graveyards of local churches. Candace couldn't imagine why anyone would want to do something like that. She loved cemeteries, especially this one. She looked out over the headstones in the dappled moonlight and thought it magical.

Candace's mom called her interests morbid. Of course, mom had to take some of the blame. She was the one who had first exposed Candace to films like *The Corpse Bride*, *Beetlejuice* and *The Nightmare Before Christmas*. Approaching her seventeenth birthday, Candace loved all things dark and Gothic.

There were a few of girls at Wellman High School who were sort of Goth, but Candace didn't really like any of them. She was lucky to have found Austen. He was the Jack Skellington to her Sally. He was a year older than she was, but acted younger. She wondered if she loved him. She was starting to think she might.

Austen led the way down the gentle slope to the iron gate which led to Amelia Bishop's grave and, of course, her statue. Candace had heard all the stories. That the statue wept tears of blood. That it went walking among the tombstones on full moons. That sometimes people heard it crying. She had been coming to the cemetery every week for almost a year and she'd never seen anything like that. She'd always found the grassy knoll where Amelia's statue stood to be a peaceful place.

With his long, lanky legs, Austen stepped over the short fence with ease. Then he opened the gate and bid Candace enter with a bow and a flourish. She couldn't help giggling. He was such a goof sometimes.

They went up the slight rise to the flat area where two tombstones stood. Candace had read the inscriptions a million times it seemed. One grave was Amelia's, of course. The other belonged to her sister Grace, who according to the stories, had never married.

"Want to ask Amelia where her babies are?" Austen said.

"God no, and don't you dare."

"I'm just kidding."

Candace smiled to show she wasn't really mad. "I know. But you know I hate the idea of people doing that. Of coming up here and taunting her."

They both sat cross-legged on the ground near the statue. Normally they liked to light a small candle, but with the increased police presence, that wouldn't be a good idea. Candace wished the clouds would clear away. The moon had gone into hiding just as they came down from their hiding place. Of course she could see the gleaming marble statue easily enough. It almost seemed to glow with its own inner light.

"I wouldn't try it tonight, anyway," Austen said. "Amelia's face looks, I don't know, different. Almost like she's angry."

"Don't be a goofus, Austen. I love her, but she's just a statue."

Still, he had a point. Somehow the way the shadows fell on the statue's face seemed to give her a stern look. Like her brows were knit, and the corners of her mouth were turned down in a scowl.

"Maybe someone's been messing with her," Austen said, uncrossing his legs and rising.

Austen stepped up close to the statue and leaned forward, turning his head slightly as he studied Amelia's face. At that moment the moon emerged from behind the clouds, and Candace had a sudden feeling that something was wrong. In the light of the moon, she could see that the statue's face really was scowling. It had changed, somehow.

The next instant one of the statue's arms shot out and grabbed Austen's jacket. Austen screamed a high-pitched wail and Candace found that she was screaming too. Amelia stretched out her other hand and grasped Austen's face. For a moment it seemed almost as if she were caressing the boy, and then she closed her hand and Candace heard Austen's jaw break. Blood and teeth were forced out of his mouth by an agonized, guttural shriek.

Candace tried to get up, but her legs wouldn't support her and she sprawled in the grass. Looking up, she saw the statue was still gripping Austen's head. With a quick twist, Amelia broke his neck. She dropped his limp body, then turned her stone face toward Candace and grinned with marble teeth.

Candace struggled to get up again and managed to stay on her feet this time. She tried to stagger away, but felt something close over her wrist. The next second she screamed yet again as the statue's hand clamped down and all the bones in her wrist were shattered and crushed.

"Oh God, stop!" Candace cried.

The statue was still grinning. Her other hand reached out for Candace's neck, the almost delicate, white fingers splayed to grasp her throat. Candace screamed some more, knowing it wouldn't help, but unable to stop.

Candace saw a shadow rise above the statue of Amelia Bishop. A dark shape, something like a man appeared behind Amelia and swarmed over the statue, wrapping it in what looked like a cloak of some sort. Candace felt the pressure release from her ruined wrist and she fell backwards onto the grass.

As she watched, the statue ceased all motion and went rigid. The shadowy form slid away, as if someone were drawing a shroud from the statue. The marble figure shuddered, and then collapsed, shattering into a shower of rubble. As the shadowy figure faded from view, Candace thought she saw a face among the swirling folds. It was the last thing she saw before she gratefully passed out.

If ever there was an area in or around Wellman, Georgia that practically screamed ghosts and apparitions, it's Crawford's Hollow. The deep valley that runs to the south and west of Wellman has a long history of violence, both before and after Wellman itself was settled.

According to old legends, the Native Americans in the area thought the land there was cursed, or diseased, and home to creatures never meant to see the world of humans. Though the exact stories are lost to time, it's easy to see why the natives might have felt that way. The area is cut deep enough into the ground that the surrounding lands seem to choke off most of the sunlight, leaving the Hollow lost in shadows and perpetual twilight at the brightest times of the day.

Several small creeks empty into the area, and while tributaries drain away a lot of the moisture, the bottom of the Hollow is filled with enough swampy regions to promise far too many mosquitoes and more than a few areas deep enough to allow for cars and human remains to vanish away forever.

It sounds like so much speculation but the area's history might beg to differ. When Prohibition became a fact of life in the United States several of the families in the Hollow started making their own moonshine to compensate for the loss of legitimate spirits. The Hollow became notorious for its distilleries, and several different revenuers managed to disappear when heading into the area, never to be seen again, at least not alive.

The federal government did not approve of having employees vanish, and did what it could to rectify the situation on December 3, 1933, two days before Prohibition was revoked.

Though exact numbers are not known, it's rumored that close to sixty men entered Crawford's Hollow, intent on ending the business of moonshiners in the area. The resulting conflict cost the Federal Bureau of Investigation several lives, and was believed at that time to have put an end to two of the more notorious families in the area. The exact numbers may never be known, but the Blackbourne family and the Tunney family were thought to have been killed off by the assault on their properties. The Blackbournes at least have since made a comeback in the area, but the Tunneys have not been seen in Wellman for decades.

Though the area has never officially been a part of Wellman proper, it's considered part of the town by local residents. The local police department is not known for frequenting the Hollow, but there is a long history of conflicts with the Brennert County Sheriff's Department, who only a few years ago removed over fifty cars from the area. In all cases the cars had long since been reported as stolen and their owners reported missing and in many cases presumed dead.

No bodies have ever been found. The list of disappearances in Crawford's Hollow is cause enough for locals to consider the area haunted, to be sure, but the actual reports of spectral activity are worse.

There have been reports of several ghostly vehicles driving down the mostly unpaved roads in the area. Documentation from the Brennert County Sheriff's Department confirms over forty different cases where people have reported cars and motorcycles alike driving into the Hollow and vanishing moments later, as well as thirteen different claims that a nearly hysterical girl dressed in in white was picked up after begging for help and claiming that she and her family had been abducted.

In all cases where the mystery girl was picked up, the same people reporting the incident also claimed that she vanished without a trace minutes later. In each instance the drivers were in the process of taking her to the sheriff's department when she disappeared.

Sometimes you just couldn't catch a break. Doug Fulford was absolutely sure that he was having one of those days. Two hours of trying to get Jolene Blackbourne to notice him had failed miserably, and that after he'd had Jeff at work swearing she put out if she was liquored up. Instead of hanging with him she'd brushed him away like lint on her collar.

Then the Mustang, his dream car, broke down a stone's throw from the absolute worst place in the world, Crawford's Hollow. The stories about the Hollow were too many to count, and all of them were bad news. Hell, most of the Blackbournes lived there and aside from Jolene there wasn't a one of them he wanted to get to know. Some of the creepiest bastards he'd ever met, and mean didn't even come close to describing them.

They were the tip of the iceberg from what he'd heard. Police did raids there and came back with horror stories. No, thanks, he could do without.

Doug thought about calling his wife, and then thought better of it. Angie was on the warpath lately, because he'd been late every night for over a week. Like he had any reason to want to get home to her. She'd be in a screaming mood for sure and he was damned if he was going to give her any reason to start in on him.

No, he'd rather walk. He could have called for a cab, or even an Uber, but he couldn't find his damned phone anywhere. Just his luck, Jolene had taken it, or maybe he'd left it at work again. Either way, he was hoofing it home.

It was raining, of course. Why wouldn't it be raining?

Fifteen minutes into the walk Doug promised himself he was going back to the gym. He'd already given up smoking, it was too damned expensive, but he was feeling every cigarette he'd ever smoked, and his breaths were ragged and his side hurt.

There had been a time when he'd been all lean muscle, but these days that was a pipe dream. He was about one slice of pie away from heart attack territory and he knew it. This was simply a reminder to do something about it.

Of course the road was on a growing incline and that helped him with his sentiment if not his predicament.

The woods to his left led down into Crawford's Hollow. They were an incentive to get his butt in gear. There was nothing about the area that didn't creep him out in the extreme. Just because he wanted to be gone, he checked his pockets again for his phone. It still wasn't where it belonged.

Something made a loud cracking noise in the woods, and Doug made himself move faster. It sounded like a very large branch breaking away from an equally large tree, but why it might be falling was what worried him. He squinted against the cold rain splashing into his eyes and licked the water trails running past his lips.

"Never again. Straight home tomorrow." It was a promise he'd made before, but he meant it as sincerely as he had the last time he'd made it.

There was a different type of thunder from behind him, and the road lit up enough to throw a long shadow stretching away from his body. Maybe he was in for a little luck after all. Doug grinned at the thought and turned to see what sort of car was coming up the road toward him. His thumb went up and to his side immediately, and despite the crappy weather he put on his best smile. He hadn't made Salesman of the Quarter three times by frowning.

The car was half a football field away, rolling slowly out of the Hollow, but even so Doug could tell it was a behemoth of a vehicle, likely from the 1950s or even earlier. They just didn't make them close to that size any longer.

Doug was not a car aficionado, but he knew a classic when he saw one, the 1947 Buick Roadmaster Hearse had once been the pride of the Tillinghast Funeral Home and Mortuary. For three years it had been the primary source for the funeral home to deliver the dead from any part of Brennert County and Wellman. Then it had vanished, never to be seen again. Both the vehicle and the driver, Edgar Tillinghast, disappeared in October of 1950, and neither were ever found.

The Hearse was back, but if there was a driver behind the wheel the glare from the headlights hid him away.

Doug's smile faded away from his round face as he watched the vehicle. There was no reason for his growing dread, merely a feeling that things were not quite right on the lonely stretch of rain-drenched road.

His hand trembled slightly as he lowered his thumb, and Doug found himself wondering if the thin pine trees along the side of the Hollow would be enough to stop the distant car as he heard the engine scream and saw the vehicle surge and withdraw like a Pitbull pulling at a heavy chain.

"Okay then…" His voice faded away as a flash of lightning turned the world around him stark white and almost immediately thunder cracked across the area, echoing off the hills and coming back with additional cracks and growls. Down the incline he could clearly see the Hearse when the lightning flashed. It was not a clean car. It was not well-preserved. There were holes in the metal skin that looked like fatal wounds, and the windows were covered in a heavy layer of murk. Thick plumes of exhaust spilled from the tailpipe, with sputtering rumbles from the engine.

The flash of light vanished and hid away the worst of the damage done to the old car.

As he looked on, the Roadmaster shivered and surged toward him again. Rubber tires that should have long since rotted away spun on the slick road, and let out a scream.

Doug let out a scream of his own as those tires caught purchase and the whole wreck tore up the road straight for him amid a cloud of smoke.

Adrenaline poured into his body and his legs moved, kicking against the wet tarmac and sending his body forward even as his blood pressure rocketed.

He thought of Angie as he ran. Sure, they fought. They had arguments all the time, but they also had moments of pure joy and those moments suddenly meant everything to him, the way they had when they were first married. Jolene Blackbourne was nowhere in his thoughts as he tried to elude the massive, derelict transport that had found him on the dark stretch of road.

He didn't have time to pray out loud or he would have.

Doug cut a hard left for the trees and very nearly dove between two of them. He'd be safe. He had to be safe. Angie was waiting for him at home, counting on him.

The trees behind him did nothing at all to stop the hearse, though they should have prevented the thing from coming close. The rusted grill caught him just above his hips and bent him backward until he felt the chilled engine under the rotting hood. The pointed end of the hood ornament sliced through the skin to the right of his spine even as the impact shattered vertebrae.

Pushed forward and then knocked down, Doug was crushed by the massive weight of the Roadmaster.

His Mustang was found on the road leading into Crawford's Hollow at 7:12 a.m. the next morning. There was no sign of any disturbance on the side of the road. Doug Fulford was reported missing by his wife, Angela, at 9:00 a.m.

His body stayed hidden away for nearly a week before Jolene Blackbourne caught the scent of decomposition and called in the location using a burner phone she kept for just such things. Doug finally caught her attention.

———

The darkness of the night was complete and palpable. Ellie Mae Hollander liked the dark. She found it comfortable and she always had. The whole of Wellman was laid out before her, and she smiled at that thought as she walked along the sidewalk next to Main Street and looked over the shops near the town square.

There were a lot of shops and over half of them were open. Some people swore up and down that Wellman, her hometown, closed as soon as the sun set, but they were wrong. You just had to know where to look. Tonight her goal was the Second Chances shop. Second Chances had a great collection of old clothes as well as a really large supply of classic old Halloween goodies, and as Halloween was just around the corner, she intended to have a little fun with the money she'd saved up.

Working part time as a waitress was hard work, but it was rewarding. She was good at her job and she didn't mind flirting. She froze up when it came to talking to people in the real world, but when she was working it was like she was a different person.

Sometimes she wished she could be that person all the time, but mostly she was okay with just being herself.

Second Chances was decorated to remind people that it was the spookiest time of the year, and Ellie Mae couldn't help smiling as she looked at the orange and black decorations. They were new, but they looked like they were from the 1960s. Grinning skulls, cackling witches and hissing black cats adorned the windows, along with gap-toothed Jack O'Lanterns and Frankenstein's Monster.

She opened the door and stepped into the smell of old books and fabric softener. The aisles were crowded with every sort of knickknack, but just now, especially, there were things made to create a perfect Halloween atmosphere. Tucker Hayes, the owner and proprietor, managed to have the best collections of seasonal stuff. What she never understood was where he hid those collections when the seasons changed.

Tucker smiled a warm welcome and left her alone. He knew her, and knew she didn't like to talk when she was shopping. She preferred to concentrate on exactly what she wanted.

Halloween music played in the old stereo system, and she bopped her head to Bobby "Boris" Pickett's "The Monster Mash," though she'd never much liked the song. It was infectious, and she let the music take her along for the ride.

There were a few other shoppers looking around. A very bored looking woman who was waiting for her son to pick out something, Mister Harper from down the street, who was nice enough but just a touch creepy with the way he eyed her, a couple of girls a few years younger than her who were going through the racks of vintage clothes. even as she drank all of them in, another man came into the building. He was plain enough in appearance, but he set off alarm bells in her head. He ignored her and she immediately returned the favor.

"The Monster Mash" ended and was replaced by "The Feast of the Mau-Mau." The bored mom switched over to an annoyed expression, but Ellie Mae liked the new song better.

Somewhere outside of the shop a powerful car engine came down the road, not purring but rumbling along with the sounds of thunder occasionally making themselves known, while Screamin' Jay Hawkins lived up to his name.

Strong hands grabbed Ellie Mae's arms and physically lifted her off the ground. She snapped her head around to see who was grabbing at her and saw the stranger who'd come in last. He said nothing, and instead moved at a fast walk, carrying her like she weighed next to nothing.

"Put me down!" It was all she could think to say.

"You got it." He tossed her a good ten feet and she landed, staggered and tried to maintain her balance.

Before she could finish her less than graceful dance to keep her feet, the front of Second Chances exploded in a hailstorm of fragmenting safety glass. The shape that came through the window was impossible to miss and completely unexpected. The massive old car looked like it shouldn't have been able to start up, let alone get moving at a serious clip, but the hearse bulled into the front of the shop and sent displays of vintage Halloween decorations sailing. A plastic pumpkin soared through the air and bounced off the kid who'd been looking at monster figures. Had it weighed more than an ounce or two it would have caved his head in. His mom let out a shriek that announced she was no longer bored or annoyed.

Les Harper let out a scream of his own as a wooden sign pointing to Halloweentown bounced from the front of the hearse and slammed him in the stomach hard enough to drop him to his knees.

The two girls who were in vintage clothes let out matching tea kettle shrieks and backed up hastily, only stopping when they ran into the counter where Tucker stared, goggle-eyed, at the oversized wreck backing away from the front of his shop.

"What the fuck?" Tucker summed up her feelings nicely.

"Ghost car," explained the man who had saved her life. "I hate ghost cars."

Without another word the stranger moved after the old hearse, stepping over fallen displays and through the shattered glass.

Ellie May stared after him for three seconds, and then followed.

Out on the street she saw the man digging in his overcoat's pockets following after the massive old hearse, which still should not have been able to move, considering its condition. It looked ancient, and it apparently didn't care that it should have been motionless.

"You should run, kid." The man didn't even look at her.

"I'm not a kid."

"Yeah, you are. You should run." He poured the contents of a small envelope into his hand, and eyed the hearse, which was revving its engine to a roaring growl. The man was smiling now, and his smile gave her a full-on case of the willies.

"Mister, that hearse is going to run you down."

"Yeah. I sort of noticed. That's why I want you elsewhere."

"You're the one who's gonna get smeared on the sidewalk." She was yelling to be heard over the tank of an old car. The whole thing was shaking, and the tires started to spin on the slick road. It came forward like a bullet, roaring away, and though it really didn't seem possible for the wrecked old thing to go anywhere, it came at the stranger. He was a dead man and she knew it.

Then he threw the dust in his hand at the hearse, and it imploded on itself. That was the only way she could put it. One second there was a hearse charging for the man and the next it shrank down and collapsed in on itself like a magic trick. Instead of getting crushed under a ton of old car, the man caught what was left of the hearse as easily as he might catch a softball.

Whatever it became, he closed it in his hand and held on tightly.

Without another word, the man started walking away.

Without another word, Ellie May started following him.

———

Sascha Wurdilec did not like Don Washington very much. He was always trying to find quick answers to the questions they needed to research, and as often as not he decided that he was right, and the rest of the world was wrong, based on very little evidence.

Also, he had the annoying habit of speaking to her breasts, instead of talking to her while looking her in the eyes. At least Mark Irvin was capable of noticing she was a person, not a sexual object.

She considered that fact while she looked at the results of her latest tests. There was nothing on the shirt that still held a bloodstain. There was nothing on the flakes of bloodied paint they'd taken from Travis's friend's apartment. According to the best science, there was simply no blood or discoloration on either of the objects and yet she could see the still damp blood, even if she couldn't wash it away.

Don would have been infuriated. She was fascinated. Here was a mystery. She wanted answers and she would take the time to find those answers. Don would rather use a Ouija board, as if those damned things could prove anything scientifically.

Both Mark and Don were supposed to join her at the farm, and then they were all going to Mark's alleged hanging tree. According to Mark he had seen the spectral images of several hanged Union soldiers, and others besides, just the other night. He thought they might show again, and she intended to be there if they did. Don was an unfortunate side effect of the discussion as he claimed the same thing. If he started in again about communing with the dead via his Ouija board, she just might have to kick his ass. It wouldn't be hard. He was large, yes, but he was soft.

She thought about the look on his face the one time he'd tried to make a move on her and repressed a shudder. Her repulsion had nothing at all to do with his size and everything to do with his personality. He genuinely disgusted her as a person.

That wasn't fair. He couldn't help being who he was. Still, she made it a point to avoid being alone with Don. He was creepy at the best of times.

The road to the Harper farm was empty of traffic, which was good considering the rain had been coming down hard enough to make driving dangerous. The other good news was the rain had finally stopped after she arrived. It was late and the farm was closed, but the Harper's had given her permission to be on their property and she parked in a gravel lot close to the roadside pumpkin patch.

Sascha climbed out of her Lexus and looked for her two fellow members of the society. She thought about Don and repressed a scowl. It might be time to see about replacing him as her second in command. She couldn't stop thinking about the things she'd heard about him trying to cast spells to make possible ghosts more active. The scientific method had nothing to do with his efforts. Moreover, she believed in ghosts already. Her mother and father were from Czechoslovakia, back before it became two separate countries, thank you very much, and she'd been raised to believe in certain things that most people took as fiction. The difference was that she intended to prove their existence, and she wanted to do it the right way. Everyone in the group seemed to understand that, except Don.

Don came her way, with Mark in tow. Both of them were smiling at her and she forced down the moderate irritation she felt. Sascha knew she was good looking. She'd even done a little modeling. She just wasn't particularly interested in dating anyone at the present time. She had a lot going on in her life. And if she were being completely honest, she also had a father with a watchful eye. Ivan Wurdilec was an overprotective man, and he was big enough to curl Don like a dumbbell.

"Hi guys," She looked away from them toward the pumpkin patch to her left and the Jack O'Lantern headed scarecrow guarding the patch. From what the Harpers had told Sascha, they'd been using the same scarecrow for years. It stood in the cornfield until that crop was harvested, and then they moved it to the pumpkin patch at Halloween for atmosphere. They replaced the thing's creepy burlap face with a freshly carved pumpkin of proper size.

Mark said, "I hope you brought your Nikon. I've got digital covered if you've got film covered."

"I brought it. I also brought along the shirt and paint samples I told you about."

"Cool! I really wanted to see those." Mark was smiling. Don was frowning and had the start of his wounded puppy expression growing on his round face. She realized she'd never mentioned the samples to him. It wasn't an intentional slight, but he might well take it as one.

How to disarm the situation? She'd come up with something. Besides, she was still seriously thinking about tearing him apart over his alleged ceremonies.

Mark's eyes grew round in his face, and the color drained from him. She'd never seen a man go pale before, but she watched his skin turn the color of milk.

"Mark? Are you okay?"

Mark shook his head soundlessly. His eyes were focused beyond her. Don said, "Sascha! Don't move."

But she did move. She couldn't help it. She turned to see what the two young men were staring at. At that exact moment the scarecrow turned its head and looked at her. Sascha froze.

The straw effigy seemed to grow in size as it pulled itself free of the stake that held it. It lurched toward the trio, twig-hands spreading. The idiot grin on its face seemed to get bigger and a candle flared up inside its hollow head.

Sascha emitted a yelp and started backing away. She stumbled over a pumpkin and fell. That seemed to decide the walking horror on its choice of victims and it turned toward her.

And then Don stepped between her and the thing. He held a cross in his trembling hand. It was a big wooden affair with a crucified Christ in place.

"Leave this place!" He yelled the words and the cross shook in his tightly clenched fingers.

The scarecrow's head swiveled Don's way. Its carven mouth yawned wide and it swatted the cross aside. Don screamed in utter terror as the thing's stick-like fingers latched onto him, digging into his flesh like thorns.

"Get it off me," Don screeched. "Get it off me!"

Sascha wanted to help him. She really did. But her muscles wouldn't respond. She couldn't make herself get up. She glanced over at Mark, but he also looked frozen in place by fear.

Sascha heard a weird rustling noise and she looked back at Don and the scarecrow. In the light from the fallen light she saw thick, dark green roots sprouting up from the ground near Don's feet. They encircled his legs and climbed upward like kudzu gone mad. But these were pumpkin vines.

The vines spread across Don's corpulent form, wrapping around his torso and arms. And then, as Sascha watched in fascinated terror, the vines began to pull Don down into the soil.

"Oh God, no," Don yelled. "Help me, Mark. Oh God."

Don thrashed around, trying to pull free, but the scarecrow held him firmly until the vines had completely trapped him. Then it put its hands on his shoulders, pushing downward, as if helping the vines to drag Don down to his own private hell. His legs were completely out of sight now and he was sinking fast.

At the same time, something dark came out of the sky, descending like a crashing kite cut off from the wind, all flapping black cloth and a grotesque face. As Sascha watched, the skeletal thing latched onto the scarecrow.

Now it was the effigy's turn to scream. A hollow echoing wail escaped from the ragged mouth as the flying creature wrapped the scarecrow in the folds of its cloak. Then the scarecrow went stiff and began to fall apart. Even as the creature released the broken fragments of the scarecrow, it turned its face toward Sascha, and she saw that its skull like face still had human eyes in its sockets.

The sight of those eyes broke Sascha's paralysis, and she made herself get up. She was barely on her feet as the cowled thing reached for her with a hand from which the flesh was mostly rotted away, leaving exposed bone and gristle.

Sascha dodged away and ran toward Mark. She grabbed his arm and said, "We have to get out of here!"

Mark screamed and shook her off, but at least he was moving. He seemed to notice the dark specter for the first time and he turned and ran.

Sascha spared one last look back at Don. He was almost completely underground now, with just his head sticking up among the pumpkins. But his eyes. Oh God, he was still alive.

Then the skeletal creature flowed toward her again and that was it for Sascha. She had thought herself braver than that, but she turned on her heel and joined Mark in running for dear life.

She had never been so afraid in her entire life.

Sascha, who had been a track star in high school and who still ran a couple of miles every other day, ran right past Mark and never looked back. She cried as she ran, afraid for herself, afraid for Mark, and though she was barely aware of it, grieving for Don, who she'd thought of as a friend despite himself. In the end he had tried to save her and she had run away and left him to die.

"Seriously, Carter," Cindy said, "I don't know how much more of this I can take."

Decamp said, "You said on the phone you'd had more of those phantom pains."

They were sitting in Decamp's study. Outside, a cold October rain was slapping against the windows, sending rivulets cascading down the glass. Cindy was glad to be in Decamp's house, which was warm and somehow managed to be cozy, even with the study's rather macabre décor. It was fairly early in the morning, but the visions had been really bad this time and Decamp had told her to come right over when she'd called.

Cindy said, "Yes, in my jaw and my hand this time."

Decamp said, "There was another death last night in the Methodist cemetery."

"Jesus. What happened?"

"A young man was killed, his jaw broken and many of his bones crushed. His girlfriend almost suffered the same fate and one of her wrists was severely injured. She hasn't given a full statement yet, but apparently she said she and the boy were attacked by the statue of Amelia Bishop, the same statue you thought had moved."

"Good Lord. Is the statue back in the same position now?"

"It was destroyed. The young woman said a ghostly figure in robes shattered it somehow."

"Like those things at Emily's house."

"Yes. Your phantom pains mimic some of the injuries the young people had. I have to say, Cindy, your seeming connection with this is disturbing."

"Imagine how I feel. It all started after I touched Harrington's tombstone. Before that I was just having some weird feelings, but now it's like something is targeting me."

Decamp said, "Something very well may be."

Cindy suppressed a shudder. "What do you mean, Carter?"

Decamp got up from his desk and went to a coffee maker in one corner and refilled his mug. Then he brought the carafe over to Cindy and topped off her cup. "A pattern has emerged in these killings. They originally seemed random, but now that so many people have died, it's evident each of the deaths is somehow connected to a local legend. Civil War meatball surgery in the Wellman House. The moving statue. It's almost as if all the urban legends and ghost stories are coming true all at once."

"But what has that got to do with me?"

Decamp resumed his seat. "I'm not sure. I think there is some guiding force behind all of this, but I've no idea what it is. I also think it has a purpose. An agenda you somehow seem to have tapped into."

"I knew I never should have gone back to Wellman."

"It is a singular place to be sure."

"Okay, so say this is all connected to Wellman folklore. What do we do about it?"

"Later this morning I have an appointment with the acting head of the Wellman Historical Society. I'm going to see if I can gather some more information about William Avery Harrington and his circle. This situation began at Harrington's grave, so that seems a likely line of investigation."

"Is Charon going with you?"

"Not this time. She'll be on her way to the Atlanta airport by then. She's taking Wade Griffin to catch a flight. I'm sure you remember Griffin."

She remembered Wade Griffin all right. Six feet four inches, and probably the most dangerous human being she'd ever met. He was a private detective, but Cindy knew he also worked as a mercenary sometimes. He was probably flying off to some place no sane person would go.

"Oh yeah. That is one memorable guy. Do you want me to go along with you then?"

"Under normal circumstances I'd love to have you along, but for right now, I think you should stay out of Wellman."

"You're probably right, but I'd really like to go anyway."

Decamp raised an eyebrow. "Is there a particular reason, my dear?"

"You said yourself, whatever is going on, it seems to be targeting me. I don't like threats, Carter. I'm not hiding from this."

Decamp didn't answer right away, and for a moment, Cindy thought he was going to insist that she stay behind. Then he said, "We have some time before we need to leave for Wellman. How about I cook some breakfast. I've been told my omelets are excellent."

"That would be great."

Chief Dave Braxton always thought the Brennert County medical examiner's building looked like a 1960s era dentist's office, with its brown brick exterior and low, flat design. There was talk of a new building but that had been going on for years. The City of Wellman used the old coroner system, and had no morgue or autopsy facilities, so bodies went to the county office or the GBI crime lab in Decatur.

Though the office was technically closed at seven in the evening, Ron Pang had let Braxton know he would be working late. Braxon parked in the NO PARKING area at the front of the building, even though the lot was empty except for Pang's car. It was good to be chief.

He found Pang in his office, head down over a stack of papers, his thin, pale face bathed in the baleful glow of the computer monitor. Pang looked up as Braxon came in.

"Tell me you brought beer," Pang said.

Braxton held a six pack aloft. "Bass Ale. Only the finest."

"You're a saint."

"Tell my ex that. While you're at it, got anything to tell me about the Oden kid?"

Pang leaned back in his chair. "You want the official report or what I actually think?"

"Tell me what you think first."

"Okay. As crazy as it sounds, the injuries line up with what the girl told you."

Braxton winced at the thought of his conversation with Candace. It had been midafternoon when she'd finally been lucid enough to talk, and Braxton had needed to be very gentle with her. She still ended up working herself up so much that she had to be sedated again. But before that she had told him the statue of Amelia Bishop had come to life and attacked both her and Austen.

Braxton said, "Her name's Candace."

"Yeah. Austen Oden's jaw was shattered by pressure. Same with Candace's arm. Like a vise, or a hand of stone had tightened around them. But no one's going to believe that."

"Damn. So what's your official report going to say?"

"The damage could have been inflicted by blunt trauma, even though I don't think it was. Someone with a mallet or sledgehammer could have attacked the kids, and shattered the statue."

"Yeah, the powers that be will like that. It's nice and neat. If it makes you feel better, the attending physician at the hospital agreed with you. He said Candace's arm had been crushed. He suggested maybe the kids were messing around with the statue and it toppled over on them, killing Austen and injuring Candace."

Pang said, "And then it jumped off them and shattered itself in a fit of guilt."

"Be sure and put that in your report."

"I will. Give me a beer." Braxton did so. Pang took a long pull. "What the hell is going on here, Dave? Between Walter Lathem being cut to pieces, those boys in the cemetery, and all the other weird stuff going on, I don't know what to think."

Braxton took a drink from his own bottle. "How long you lived in Wellman?"

"Close to ten years."

"So you know odd things happen here. But you didn't grow up here like I did. As a kid I saw things in the woods at night that my adult mind tells me I imagined. But I know I didn't. We've always had more than our share of urban legends and things that just couldn't be explained.

"I've had some late-night drinking talks with Sheriff Carl Price, and that guy has seen some shit. He won't talk about it much, but there's some freaky stuff in this county."

"So you think I should tell the powers that be what I really think?"

"Hell no. The people who run things here tend to be from old families. They might believe you, but they'd never admit it. More than once they've had to turn a blind eye to things they couldn't explain in a rational way."

"I get the idea you saw something else at the cemetery, Dave."

"Yeah, though nobody's talking about it. The patrol guys who found the kids probably saw it. I *know* the crime scene guys saw it."

"Saw what?"

Braxton shook his head. "Footprints. Deep, deep footprints. Something would have to be seriously heavy to make prints like that."

"Like a statue," Pang said.

"Exactly like that."

PART III

For a town with so much weirdness, Wellman certainly took to Halloween. Cindy noted all the decorations as she and Decamp crossed the town square. There was an assortment of freestanding dummies, dressed in various costumes. These were apparently sponsored by local businesses and schools. In addition to vampires and ghosts, there was a dummy in doctor's scrubs, and one in a Wellman High football uniform. A farmer over there. A cheerleader over here. They were meant to be cheerful, but given what she knew of the mobile statue, the life-size effigies gave Cindy the creeps just now.

In addition to the figures, the square was decorated with bales of hay, rows of pumpkins, and yards of hanging spider webs. Strings of lights ran around the central gazebo and stretched across the streetlights. It would probably look pretty and suitably spooky at night. A nice place to walk arm in arm with a boyfriend, blithely unaware that there really were evil spirits and demons abroad in the night.

They went up the steps to the front of the Wellman House. The place was still officially closed, but a middle-aged woman in a dark dress stood just inside the double doors, and unlocked them as Cindy and Decamp approached.

"Good morning, Professor," the woman said as she swung one door open and beckoned the pair inside.

"Good morning, Janice. This is my associate, Cindy Kane. Cindy, this is Janice Cantrell."

"Nice to meet you," Cindy said.

"And you," said Janice, locking the door behind them. "Though I wish it were under better circumstances. After what happened to Walt, we're all pretty shaken up. I only got here half an hour ago and I won't be staying after you two leave."

"We won't take up much of your time," Decamp said. "As I told you on the phone, I'm just looking for information about William Avery Harrington."

"I've gathered a few things, professor, and they're in my office."

Janice led them down a short hallway to a group of offices. Cindy noticed that Decamp was allowing Janice to call him "professor," which was unusual. He was retired and he generally told people just to call him by name. She suspected he was taking advantage of his title to get the information he needed. Decamp had also let slip that he was a patron of the museum and donated quite a bit of money to the place every year.

Janice's office was small and neat. Cindy and Decamp took chairs in front of her desk. Janice handed Decamp a file folder as she took her seat.

"Some documents you'll probably want to look over. Copies of Harrington's will, deeds and such. There's also a thumb drive in there with articles from the *Wellman Tribune* dating back to Harrington's time."

"You're a treasure, Janice," Decamp said with an incline of his head.

Cindy knew Decamp had probably already uncovered most of that material on his own, but he was always polite and often charming.

Janice smiled. "I have something else you'll find of interest, I think, but we'll come to that. How much do you already know about Harrington?"

Decamp said, "From what I've read he started as a plantation manager near the coast."

"That's correct. He ran rice and cotton plantations in the St. Simon's area for a man named Butler."

Decamp said, "Eventually he made enough money to buy his own property and he and his family settled near Cedar Creek, in what would become Wellman. He decided the proximity to running water would be a good place for a cotton mill, and since he already had contacts in the cotton industry, he set up shop here."

"Right on every count. Harrington dammed the creek to generate power for his mill. He was extremely successful and invited some of his friends in the cotton industry to move here and build homes." Janice consulted a slip of paper on her desk. "Samuel Penobscot, Thaddeus Burke, and several others. And that's where things turn a bit weird."

Cindy said, "Oh?"

"Yes, it seems that Harrington and his buddies formed a sort of secret society. Something like the Masonic Order, I suppose, but some of the local stories make it sound more sinister. Late-night meetings dressed in robes, and such."

"Dark monks," said Decamp.

"What?"

"Just musing," said Decamp.

Janice nodded. "Anyway, that brings me to my last discovery. The one I think will really interest you, professor. After what happened to Walt, the police made a mess of the basement floor, which I completely understand. But while we were cleaning up, we found something in a back corner. Years ago, the Harrington family renovated Harrington Hall and they gave the museum a bunch of William Avery Harrington's possessions, a lot of which got put into storage."

Decamp leaned slightly forward in his chair. "What did you find?"

Janice grinned. "A trunk. I haven't really had time to go through it, but it's obviously his property. It's full of personal papers and such. I thought you might like to have a look at it."

"I certainly would."

"It has to be off the record, though," Janice said. "The board members would have a fit if they knew I let you see it before the contents had been cataloged."

"I shall observe every due caution, my dear,"

"I've no doubt of that. I hope you won't mind if I don't show you down to the basement. Right now, I really can't stand to go down there if I don't have to. That's another reason I haven't had a close look at the trunk. I'll probably have it brought up later, once the police clear the building."

"I understand completely, Janice. Cindy and I will find our own way. I've been in that part of the building before."

With that, Decamp rose from his chair. Cindy could tell he was in a hurry to see the trunk. She wasn't sure she shared his eagerness to visit the room where the gruesome murder had occurred, but she was determined to push on.

When they were out of the office, Cindy said, "Doesn't this seem just a little too big a coincidence? Harrington's trunk turning up just as all this is happening?"

"Perhaps," said Decamp. "But things like that do happen. I've seen my share of odd coincidences, both fortuitous and otherwise."

Cindy followed Decamp down another hallway to an elevator. She could feel her heart rate picking up. She did *not* want to go downstairs.

As if reading her thoughts, Decamp said, "You don't have to go down there, Cindy."

"In for a penny," said Cindy.

Decamp nodded and pressed the elevator button. The doors slid open so suddenly that it made Cindy jump. *Come into my parlor, said the spider to the fly.* They stepped into the small elevator and the cage went down.

Just as the doors opened, Cindy thought she head a whispering in her ear. A voice saying, "They all must come off." She glanced over at Decamp. He didn't show any signs of having heard anything. Just her then.

The basement smelled of antiseptic, doubtless from the crime scene cleanup. Cindy didn't see anything weird. She wasn't immediately assaulted by any odd feelings. So far, so good. Decamp found the lights and turned them all on, dispersing the shadows. He looked around and then spotted the trunk.

"In this case, Cindy," Decamp said, "I am going to insist you don't touch anything. Given your reaction to Harrington's tombstone, I really don't think you should come into contact with any of his actual possessions just now."

"No argument from me, Carter."

Decamp nodded and crossed to the trunk. He knelt down and opened the lid, which creaked so sharply it reminded Cindy of nails on a chalkboard. Nothing sprang out, though, she half expected something would.

As Decamp began rummaging through the trunk, Cindy again heard the whispering voice. It seemed closer this time, and she turned, thinking she might find someone standing beside her. There was nothing there, but the recently activated lights seemed to dim for just a moment, and then the room around her wavered and changed.

"They all must come off!" A voice screamed from close by. "All of them!"

Decamp and the trunk were gone, replaced by a group of men clustered around a table. The floor was covered with sawdust and Cindy felt her gorge rise as she saw numerous recently severed human limbs were strewn in the bloody dust. She took an involuntary step back and bumped into the elevator doors. They should have opened automatically but they didn't.

The four men at the table turned at the sound, and now Cindy could see there was someone lying on the table, and one of the men, a white-haired scarecrow, was sawing the man's leg off with an old-fashioned bone saw. He wore a bloodstained leather apron over an antiquated smock of some sort. His hands and forearms were covered with blood.

"Ah, another patient!" the white-haired man said. "This one's almost done. Bring her, men. You know all of them must come off!"

Cindy looked about for the stairwell door. There had to be stairs. But she didn't see it. The entire room behind the operating table was wreathed in mist and darkness. The "doctor's" three assistants were coming toward her, their mouths pulled back in rictus grins.

Cindy moved to her right and tried to dodge past the man on that side, but he caught her arm and gripped with such strength she felt the limb go numb. Then the other two men were on her, grabbing her, and pulling her toward the table. They turned her so she could see the doctor dump his most recent patient, now an armless, legless ruin, into the sawdust. Then her captors were lifting her and placing her on the blood-smeared table surface.

Cindy thrashed around, knowing what was coming and knowing she couldn't get away. Her arms and legs were pinned by the burly "orderlies." She saw the doctor hold up the bone saw, still covered with gore and bits of bone.

"All of them must come off," the doctor whispered in her ear.

Cindy screamed as the doctor grabbed her armed and pulled it out straight.

A second later, the doctor gave a yelp as he was suddenly pulled backward. Cindy turned her head and saw the Carter Decamp had grabbed the doctor by the back of his smock and dragged him away from the table. She saw the glimmer of Decamp's sword and then it was the doctor's head that had to come off. The white-haired man's body seemed to crumple in on itself as it fell.

The three orderlies released Cindy and started toward Decamp. Cindy saw the sword move in a blur and then it had entered one of the orderly's eyes and come out the back of his skull. Cindy rolled off the table and staggered away toward the elevator door.

The remaining two men were circling Decamp, looking for an opening, when the room was filled with an ear-piercing shrieking noise. Cindy saw two wraith-like figures appear from the shadows. They had skulls for faces, though she could see living eyes within the sockets.

Each of the creatures dug bony claws into one of the orderlies and the bulky men faded from view, their mouths wide open in silent screams. The skull-faced things vanished too, and in an instant, the basement was back to normal. Cindy rushed to Decamp.

"Oh God, Carter. Are you all right?"

"I'm fine, my dear. I'm sorry it took me so long to find you. I was digging around in the trunk and turned and you were gone."

"Don't apologize. You found me just in time. If you hadn't...Jesus, God. Can we get out of here now?"

"We certainly can. The rest of the things in Harrington's trunk can wait. I think I found what we were looking for anyway."

Decamp hefted a small, leather-bound book. Cindy said, "Is it a diary?"

"Not precisely. I'll tell you about it on the way home. I'll have to smuggle it past Janice, but it may contain information that will help us."

There are places around Wellman and the surrounding Brennert County where the phrase "light of day" is almost a myth. There are spots between some of the local mountains where the sun barely ever shines because the shadows from the mountains hide everything away. Crawford's Hollow is one such place, but another is simply called "Moon-Eyes Gap." The Gap is well known to some people. Back in the long-ago days of mining in the area Moon-Eyes Gap was home to a successful silver mine until a collapse brought the place down. According to some legends the "Moon-Eyes" dwelled in the area and destroyed the silver mine. Moon-Eyes were the local fairies or bogeymen, pale things with bulging eyes that glowed in the dark. According to the tales they would hunt down people foolish enough to get caught in the darkness, and sometimes they would find lonely women to impregnate against their will.

There are other legends about the Gap, not the least of which is the story of Hester Blackbourne, allegedly a witch who had a Moon-Eye as a familiar and who sold spells and curses to make her living in the shadow-haunted hills outside of Wellman proper.

There are tales of Hester summoning vengeance demons to do her bidding after her son was murdered by the locals for stealing young girls to be his slaves. Naturally several of the tales go into lurid details but not all of them.

According to the recorded notes from several different local sources, but not the local newspapers, it took a dozen strong men to first tie down and then hang the witch's son. He was dragged across town behind a horse and then strung up by the neck from the local hanging tree where several Union soldiers had already allegedly met a dark fate.

The end result is that after enough people heard the tales of how a demon was sent out into Wellman to hunt down the people who'd lynched Ezekiel Blackbourne, a crowd of locals allegedly stormed the Gap searching for Hester to make her put an end to the demon she'd summoned.

This much is verified by different sources: On October 31, 1891, twenty-seven men stormed into Moon-Eye Gap to put an end to Hester Blackbourne.

This much is verified: Neither Hester nor the local mob were ever seen again.

According to local legends, the Witch of Moon-Eye Gap still haunts the area, waiting for anyone foolish enough to move into the shadowed hills where her old cabin rests buried under a thick layer of ivy almost impossible to find in the summer months, but identifiable as a hut if a person knows what to look for when autumn and winter come around.

Of course, there are also rumors of active stills and moonshiners up in those hills, so most people are wise enough to stay away, even if they don't believe in witches and ghosts.

"This is Jonathan Crowley. What can I do for you?" It was the kid who'd called him into the area, Mark something or other.

"Don is dead!" He was crying. "A scarecrow came alive and attacked us and then this thing came out of the sky, and we ran! I can't go back there, Mister Crowley. I can't!"

Don Washington was the man he'd already promised himself the pleasure of torturing over summoning the dead things. Pity. He'd been looking forward to making the stupid bastard cry, and possibly, just possibly killing him and now the monsters had done it for him.

He couldn't say that, of course. The man on the phone was already in tears.

"Where are you Mark, and where did this happen?"

"It was at the pumpkin patch at the Harper's farm."

"Where is the Harper's farm, Mark? I don't know this area."

The girl following behind him said, "I know where that is," but he ignored her. He wanted more information from the man who'd summoned him here in them first place.

It took three minutes to get an address from Mark and someone named Sascha. The entire conversation took place while he was being followed by the girl from the secondhand shop where he'd taken out the ghost car, which even now was burning against his hand, desperate to be released, but no, he had plans for the thing. It was bait for whatever was happening around him, because he had a strong notion that he was dealing with at least one hungry ghost.

There was a preposterous amount of spectral activity in the area, but he could feel some of it concentrating in different locations, and he needed to find out if those locations were connected.

They had to be, because hungry ghosts could be hellish in their own right and there were at least five of them if what he was sensing was accurate. If they were connected, possibly they could be eliminated together. If not, he was in for one hell of a turbulent time.

"Who was that on the phone?" He turned and looked over his shoulder. It was the girl from the pawn shop.

"What the hell is it to you?"

"There's no reason to be rude."

"There's no reason to be polite to someone stalking after me like I'm going to answer all her questions. Go away."

"I don't want to. I want answers."

"Go google some questions. I'm not an information booth." He shook his head. The lack of manners confused him. Back when he'd been a teacher he might well have been amused, but these days he was simply annoyed.

"Now you're just being a dick." She shook her head and glared.

"It's what I do. I ignore rude little girls, and I'm a dick." He had to admit she was growing on him. At least she was willing to defend herself from cranky old monster hunters. "Just tell me what's going on."

"I'm hunting ghosts, and doing my best to ignore you. I have to say the ghosts are easier to handle."

"Still a dick."

"Still ignoring you."

She was still following him when he reached the farm. He found Mark and the girl Sascha, waiting at the edge of the property. Neither of them paid him the least bit of attention. They were too busy looking at the farm.

"It killed Don." Those were the first words from Mark.

The woman with him—and Crowley was absolutely certain he'd seen her before. He thought she might be a model, but he wasn't particularly interested in that fact and so he let it go—nodded her head. "I called Travis. He's got an expert coming with him."

Crowley rolled his eyes. "Wonderful. Just what I always wanted. An expert to help me solve the riddle of the dead ghosthunter."

"Seriously, you're a dick."

"Okay, kid. I get it, you don't like me. Now shut up. I'm busy."

"Ellie Mae?" Sascha looked at the girl following Crowley. "What are you doing here?"

"She's aggravating me. Can either of you show me where Don was attacked?"

"Sascha. This guy sucked a ghost hearse into his hand. I mean, like a real ghost. He's freaky."

"Did your parents actually name you Ellie Mae? Like *The Beverly Hillbillies*?" Crowley shook his head in mock amazement. "How to know you're in the boonies."

"Dick."

Sascha pointed toward a distant wooden post jammed into the ground. "Over there, near where the scarecrow was. That thing moved earlier. It came after us, and I think it killed Don." Her voice was very small and her eyes were very wide.

Crowley turned off the sarcasm for a moment. "What happened then, Sascha?"

"This thing with a skull for a face came down out of the sky. It wrapped around the scarecrow and killed it somehow. And we ran. We just ran away and left Don. It may still be there."

"Don't worry. If it does anything, I'll stop it."

The girl from the secondhand shop nodded solemnly. "Sucked a car into his hand. Seriously. Freakiest thing I ever saw."

"It wasn't a real car, Ellie Mae. It was a ghost."

"Still creepy."

"Then why are you following me, seriously?"

"Because like the guy from *The X Files*, I want to believe."

"Yeah, well, seeing is believing." Without another word Crowley headed for the scarecrow's former location.

It took him a moment to spot Don Washington. Most of the man was buried in the ground, only his head showed clearly, as the rest of him had been buried in the rich soil and covered with vines. All that showed looked like a pumpkin with five o'clock shadow. The man's face was slack, the mouth open and the eyes rolled back in his head. That he was dead was a given.

"Well, you don't see that every day." He looked around carefully and saw the scattered fragments of the scarecrow. They didn't move. No residual spectral energies. Whatever might have possessed the thing, it was gone now.

The hungry ghost was not. It dropped from the darkening skies with a loud shriek and Crowley saw it, acknowledged that it was not a standard haunt of any sort, and released the ghost car he'd kept trapped in the palm of his hand, throwing the small knot of energy the same way he might toss a softball. As he let go, he also removed the spell that kept the spirit trapped in a sphere of stasis.

There wasn't much to see. The energies cracked briefly and then the dark hooded form was on it, attacking with the voracity of a piranha going after a morsel of bloodied beef.

Bait for the trap.

Crowley worked as quickly as he could, weaving the same spell he'd used to capture the ghostly hearse. The energies wrapped around the dark specter and tightened like a net pulling in on a freshly captured rabbit, and the hooded thing fought back, shrieking, howling out its rage before he had a chance to pull it in closer and once again trap the energies in the palm of his hand.

The ghost car had been stronger than a regular ghost, and the hooded thing was far more powerful than the hearse had been. It burned like a coal against his hand and seared his skin but he healed as quickly as he was scalded and ignored the discomfort.

He was used to it. Another incantation uttered under his breath, and Crowley cast the energies into the afterlife. He had no idea for certain if the spirit was bound for heaven, hell, or somewhere else entirely but it was banished from the realms of the living, and that was the part that mattered.

One small threat of several, eliminated, but he doubted the trick would work that easily twice. He could sense another of the things lurking, watching him, and suspected they attacked in groups.

The dead sometimes learned quickly. He'd figured that out a very long time ago.

As he contemplated, the hooded shape stayed well out of his easy range, drifting like a kite in the windless air above him, eyes glaring hatred as it rose slowly higher and higher into the air.

Yes, whatever they were, he suspected they were working together and serving one master. A school of piranha answering to a shark, as it were. The thought was disturbing and oddly exciting. Here was something new, something decidedly different. He was seldom unsettled by the supernatural these days, and almost never excited by the challenges he faced after countless years of fighting against threats that had long since become very nearly common place.

Crowley saw the gleam of headlights and then two cars drawing closer and slowing down. One vehicle was a beat-up, old Toyota while the other was a shiny, late-model BMW. Both cars pulled into the gravel lot.

A young man and woman clambered out of the Toyota, and as Crowley watched, an unexpected surprise stepped from the BMW, a dapper man wearing a suit and carrying a cane he did not need.

Despite his preference to work alone, Crowley was pleased. It had been a while since he had seen Carter Decamp, a man he considered a peer in a calling that had very few he'd ever think of as his equal. Decamp was accompanied by an attractive young black woman.

Crowley grinned and headed toward the gathering of people looking in his direction.

"Carter Decamp, as I live and breathe. Now things should get interesting."

Though the situation was a grim one, Carter Decamp displayed a small smile when he saw Crowley. He stepped forward, hand extended. "Jonathan. You should have let me know you were in town."

Crowley said, "I meant to, Carter, but things got out of hand, as you can see."

"Yes, Travis, one of Sascha's friends, called and told me one of their friends was dead."

Crowley pointed toward a pumpkin patch beyond the gravel lot. "He's over there, buried in the ground up to his neck. I'm not sure exactly what happened yet."

A very pretty blonde woman, who Decamp assumed to be Sascha Wurdilec, said, "Vines came up from the ground and dragged Don down. It was horrible. He was screaming. I didn't…"

Emily hurried to Sascha and embraced her.

Decamp said, "It's all right, my dear. I'm sure there was nothing you could have done."

Travis said, "So it's true. Don's really dead. Jesus."

"It looks that way. Jonathan and I will go and see what we can determine."

Travis said, "I want to see him."

Decamp said, "None of you are going to see him. In just a few hours this farm is going to be a crime scene. I want all of you to stay on the gravel and don't touch anything. There's nothing we can do about Sascha and Mark but I don't want any of the rest of you involved."

Travis looked chastened but nodded his agreement. The young man Decamp assumed was Mark never looked up. He had been leaning against an old Ford truck, staring at the ground since Decamp had arrived.

"Carter," Cindy said. "I'm getting a faint impression. Something like what I felt in the museum basement."

Crowley said, "Ah, a psychic. You would be Cindy Kane. I've worked with your father. There was something here earlier. An entity of some sort. Black robe. Face like a skull. Really nasty."

Decamp said, "We've run across some of its brethren."

Crowley said, "The plot thickens. Come on. I'll show you the human pumpkin."

Decamp saw Travis wince. He knew Jonathan used sarcasm as a defense mechanism. But it could be off-putting to those who didn't know him well.

Decamp followed Crowley to the pumpkin patch. Something whitish gleamed dully in the scant moonlight among the orange gourds. Decamp stopped a few feet away and crouched down. Don Washington's head, swathed in vines, leered up at him as if growing there.

Decamp said, "It's like the ground opened up and then closed around him."

Crowley said, "According to Sascha, that's exactly what happened. From what I can tell, he was still alive during most of it. I think one of the entities finished him off. It had already destroyed the scarecrow."

"That fits the established pattern. The entities, Travis calls them skull-phantoms, seem to be seeking out things carrying eldritch energies and absorbing them. The scarecrow, a living statue, and other local urban legends."

"The kid was probably carrying some of that himself. He'd been making some ill-advised attempts at arcane rituals."

Decamp said, "So I was told. He apparently released something without meaning to."

"Any idea what?"

"Perhaps. We should probably discuss it somewhere else, though. Why don't we meet at my home in an hour or so."

"Sounds good. What about the kiddies?"

"I have a plan for them."

Together the two men walked back to the group. They were talking in hushed tones, except for Mark who still stood alone and silent. The young people turned toward Decamp and Crowley.

Decamp said, "Here is what we are going to do. Mark and Sascha will have to talk to the sheriff when he arrives. You two can't simply leave because the Harpers knew you were coming here. I'm going to advise that you edit the events just a bit. Sascha, you and Mark came together and Don arrived before you. You found him in the ground like he is now. You have no idea what happened. The rest of us were never here."

Sascha said, "But that's not what happened. Don came with Mark."

"No one knows that but you. You can tell the truth if you want to, but it will go easier if you use my version, trust me."

The young woman Travis had called Ellie Mae said, "Wait a second. What if the cops go all *CSI*? My footprints are in the mud."

Decamp said, "That's not the sort of physical evidence I'm concerned about, my dear. This is a public place. Literally hundreds of people have tromped through the pumpkin patch in the last few weeks."

"Decamp," Travis said. "How do you know the sheriff is coming?"

"Because I'm going to call him. The Wellman PD has already been looking into some of this, but the sheriff can do more damage control, so best he be the first on the scene."

"How do you know that?" Sascha said.

"We've worked together before. Don't mention me when he gets here, however." Decamp reached in a pocket and pulled out his cell. He punched a button and waited for the number he called to ring several times. "Sheriff Price. This is Carter Decamp. Sorry to wake you, but I need to make an anonymous tip."

"William Avery Harrington," Jonathan Crowley said, thumbing through the book Decamp had acquired at the museum. It had turned out to be more of a commonplace book than a journal, but it did include, not only spells and rituals, but a record of various meetings of Harrington's secret society and their actions.

Decamp said, "Yes, it was the disturbing of his grave that set all this into motion. The boy, Don, apparently used a cobbled together group of spells he thought would 'agitate' ghosts and somehow released something unexpected."

Crowley, Decamp and Cindy Kane were in Decamp's study. After leaving Sascha and Mark at the Harper farm, the rest of the group had dispersed before the sheriff arrived.

Crowley had arrived about half an hour after Cindy and Decamp got back to Marietta. Cindy found Crowley vaguely disturbing, though she couldn't say why. He had mentioned he'd worked with her father, but dad had never told her anything about him.

Crowley took one of the chairs in front of Decamp's desk. "The late Mr. Washington and I had a chat. He apparently used every spell that came to hand from various sources. Kid was an idiot."

Decamp said, "And without knowing just what he did, it will be almost impossible for us to reverse it."

Crowley said, "It's too late anyway. I think we're dealing with a hungry ghost here, Carter. Supernatural entities don't come much nastier. Question is, is Harrington the ghost or someone else?"

"I don't think it's Harrington," Cindy said.

Crowley turned and looked at Cindy. "And why is that?"

His gaze made her uncomfortable but she plunged right in. "Both times I touched Harrington's gravestone I got impressions of anger and pain. It's the pain that makes me doubt Harington is behind these happenings. It felt as if he had been suffering for a long time."

Decamp said, "That's an interesting observation, my dear, and it does tie into something I've been thinking about. This ghost is incredibly powerful. It shunted you and me into another reality briefly in the museum basement. It made me wonder how something like that could have just been waiting in a grave all these years."

Crowley said, "We know we're dealing with multiple apparitions. The skull-phantoms are servitors for something else. They're going around collecting the eldritch energies released when Harrington broke out of his grave. That suggests those energies might have been used to keep Harrington's spirit imprisoned."

Decamp said, "I don't wish to speculate too wildly, but that could also explain the presence of the skull-phantoms at Emily Strand's home."

Cindy said, "You've lost me."

"Emily felt something had followed her home from the cemetery the night of the ritual. What if it was Harrington's spirit? The ghost took her backward glance as an invitation, which allowed it to leave the graveyard. The skull-phantoms weren't looking for Emily. They were looking for Harrington, who had escaped their master's prison."

Cindy said, "Then who is the hungry ghost?"

"Might I borrow Harrington's book, please, Jonathan?" Decamp said. Crowley handed him the book and Decamp turned the pages until he was close to the end. He put the book on the desk and turned it so Cindy and Crowley could see the page he'd selected. "Harington was usually very careful not to mention the actual names of the other members of his secret society but look at this one line. '"Something must be done about Crawford."'

"Any idea who he's talking about?" Cindy said.

Decamp said, "The most likely candidate is Thaddeus Crawford, a wealthy businessman of Harrington's era. They would have traveled in the same circles. It's a bit of a stretch, but I think the fact he identified Crawford by name is very telling."

Crowley said, "Hang on. Mark Irvin mentioned a Thaddeus Crawford. A relative I think. He has a bunch of journals that belonged to him. Mark said it was pretty mundane stuff, but we should probably have a look."

Decamp and Crowley talked so fast and made such amazing leaps in logic, it was hard to follow sometimes. She'd never seen anyone who could keep up with Decamp before now. The two men were obviously on the same wavelength.

Decamp said, "We definitely should. I was telling Cindy the incidents with the various urban legends have been very brutal, even in the case of the relatively harmless ones like the crying statue. She killed one person and injured another. The energy affecting the apparitions is malignant in the extreme. However, the incidents do seem to be tapering off now."

Crowley said, "I agree. To me that signals the entity has regained much of the power it lost when Harrington escaped."

Decamp said, "Just in time for Halloween."

"The time when the veils grow the thinnest," Crowley said. "Whatever this thing's endgame is, it won't be long. I'll talk to Irvin and get the journals."

Decamp said, "I'd like to take Cindy to the Strand house and see if she can get any impression of Harrington there. That is, if you're willing, Cindy."

"I'm certainly willing, if not exactly eager," Cindy said. "Could I rest a bit first? It's like three in the morning."

Decamp said, "Of course my dear. You can use one of my guest rooms. You're welcome to use one of them as well, Jonathan."

Crowley shook his head. "I don't want to waste any more time. Besides, I do my best work in the dark."

"I just can't believe Don's really dead," Emily said as Travis killed the Toyota's engine. She had been saying variations of the same thing over and over on the drive back from the Harper's farm.

"I know," Travis said. "I have to keep reminding myself it's true."

Travis got out of the car and walked around to the other side to open Emily's door. It wasn't all from chivalry. That door tended to stick in damp weather.

"You're coming in, right?" Emily said.

"Of course. I told you I wouldn't leave you here by yourself."

They went up the front walk and Travis's gaze was automatically drawn to the roof. Nothing hung in the air outside Emily's room. Emily unlocked the front door and Travis entered first. He turned the lights on and gave a quick look around the living room, though he didn't know exactly what he was looking for. Emily came in and carefully locked the front door, checking it twice to make sure it was locked. They were both probably going to be paranoid for the rest of their lives.

"I should probably go to bed, but I'm wide awake," Emily said.

"Same," said Travis. Plopping down on the couch. He was surprised when Emily sat down right beside him, close enough that their shoulders were touching.

"What are we going to do, Travis?" Emily said. "This has all gotten so crazy and I hate feeling so out of control."

For a moment, Travis considered putting his arm around the girl, but no, he wasn't going to take advantage of her being in shock. He said, "Not much we can do. We'll have to wait and see what Decamp finds out."

Emily said, "That other guy, Crowley, he creeps me out."

"He's definitely intense. But Decamp seems to trust him. Listen, why don't we watch a movie or something, since neither of us seems to want to sleep. Try to pretend things are normal for a while."

"Okay, but nothing scary."

Emily grabbed two remotes and handed them to Travis. While he started bumping around various streaming services, Emily retrieved a throw blanket from an easy chair, and resuming her seat, she threw it over the both of them.

"How about *Star Wars*. That's not scary."

"Perfect. That's always been a comfort movie for me. I've watched it with Dad a lot."

Travis started the movie and neither of them said anything for a while. About the time the two droids were climbing into the escape pod he felt Emily's head on his shoulder. Travis glanced over at her. She was asleep. Travis had often imagined such moments with Emily. Of course those daydreams hadn't included dead friends and homicidal ghosts.

Don had been a difficult guy to like sometimes, but he hadn't deserved to die like that. Or maybe he had. His "spell" had released something that had been the cause of many deaths. Travis still hadn't come to terms with his own involvement in the carnage following the ritual. Maybe if he and the others hadn't agreed to Don's crazy scheme, Don wouldn't have gone through with it. Maybe if he had...

Travis snapped awake at the sound of someone knocking on the front door. He was disoriented for a moment, but then remembered where he was and how he'd gotten there. Sunlight streamed in through the curtains. The TV showed only a screensaver.

"What's going on?" Emily said in a sleepy voice.

"Someone at the door."

Travis gently disengaged himself from Emily and slid from under the blanket. He crossed the room and looked through the peephole in the front door. Carter Decamp stood there with Cindy Kane.

"Who is it?" Emily said.

"Decamp and the woman who came with him last night."

"Let them in and give me a couple of minutes," said Emily, ducking out of the room.

Travis opened the door. "Come in, Decamp."

"Good morning, Travis. We'll wait a few minutes before coming in. I don't know if you got a chance to talk to each other last night, but this is my friend Cindy Kane."

Travis said, "I heard her name mentioned, but no we didn't really get to talk. Hi Cindy. I'm Travis."

Cindy said, "Nice to meet you."

Decamp said, "Is Emily available to talk? I have a favor to ask."

"What sort of favor," Emily said, appearing behind Travis so abruptly he almost jumped.

"Cindy is a rather gifted psychic. Her specialty is psychometry, the ability to gather information about someone by touching something they've been in close contact with. I'd like her to come into your house and see if she can divine anything."

Emily said, "Has something changed, Carter? Do you think there's something in here?"

Decamp said, "We've learned some new information which I'll share with you soon, but yes, we think that Travis's skull-phantoms might not be interested in you, but in a spirit that has taken refuge in your home."

"Jesus," Emily said. "Sure, come on in if you think it will help."

"I'll come in now, and Cindy will join us when she's ready."

Travis said, "Is this dangerous?"

"Truthfully I don't know," Decamp said, stepping inside. "Let's move over to the far side of the living room."

They crossed the room and stood in the doorway that led to the dining room. If not for the events of the last few days, Travis would have felt ridiculous. It was a beautiful fall morning, and outside Travis could hear the sounds of the neighborhood waking up. Normal people going about normal lives.

Cindy stepped through the front door and stopped just inside. She looked around the living room and then walked a few more steps until she was near one wall. She reached out a hand and rested the tips of her fingers on the wall. She closed her eyes and leaned her head to one side as if listening intently.

Travis realized he was holding his breath. He glanced over at Emily and saw she was staring at Cindy with wide eyes. Decamp's expression was, as usual, unreadable.

Cindy took a long, shuddering breath. "Dark," she whispered. "Darkness all around."

Cindy left the wall and walked to the center of the room. She held up both hands as if feeling for something Travis couldn't see.

"Not dead," Cindy said. "I'm not dead. Oh God."

Emily said, "Is she okay?"

Decamp held up a hand for quiet, but he moved a step closer to Cindy. She was turning slowly, hands extended as if she were feeling her way through darkness.

"He must be stopped," Cindy said.

Decamp said, "Who must be stopped?"

Cindy said, "Crawford. Must be stopped. He buried me. He buried me!"

And then Cindy screamed.

The young woman swayed as if ready to fall and Decamp hurried forward. He caught her up with surprising ease for such a slender man and carried her through the front door. A moment later, Travis and Emily followed.

Cindy was leaning against Decamp's BMW. Decamp was standing close, one hand on her shoulder.

"Is she okay?" Travis called.

Cindy turned and looked at him. "I'm okay, Travis. Just need a moment."

Emily said, "There's something in my house, isn't there?"

Decamp said, "Yes, but it means you no harm. My initial supposition that an evil entity followed you home from the cemetery was incorrect. The spirit of William Avery Harrington followed you, but only to escape years of imprisonment."

"Imprisoned by what?" Travis said.

"I don't have all the answers yet," Decamp said. "But it looks more and more likely Harrington was a victim of the same entity that's causing all the weird occurrences in Wellman."

Travis said, "Maybe we should go back inside and you can explain what you've learned."

Cindy shook her head. "No way I'm going back in there. Harrington's spirit has permeated the house now. It's incredibly angry and, I think, insane. Now that I've made contact with it, I can't go back in the house."

Emily said, "How can a ghost be insane? Was Harrington crazy when he was alive?"

Cindy said, "That's just it. Harrington isn't a ghost. Not the way you mean it. He never actually died. His living spirit was ripped from him and then forced back into his body after he was buried."

"Oh God," Emily said. "You mean he's...?"

"Yes," Cindy said, "Trapped in his own grave, awake and aware for over 150 years."

It's a simple fact of life, sometimes people go missing. So far this year in the state of Georgia there are two hundred and fifty missing persons cases that are currently open and under investigation. Ten of those are open for Brennert County and the town of Wellman. Let that sink in.

That's about average for the area, where people vanish with unsettling regularity. A good number of those cases are easily resolved. There are hills and valleys around here where travelers can easily be lost and later found, and there are occasional runaways, but the percentage of cases is still unsettlingly high around these parts.

Disappearances occur all over the world, but not always in numbers quite as high as they are around Wellman and the surrounding country.

Historically speaking it has always been that way, ever since the earliest recorded days of mining in Brennert County. Truly, these hills are haunted, if not by ghosts, then by the possibility of darker things.

One of the long-standing disappearances that still haunts the area was the documented disappearance of the corpse of Thaddeus Crawford, one of the wealthiest men in Wellman during the years directly after the Civil War. Crawford, after whom Crawford's Hollow was named, and who was, in his time, one of the most powerful men in Brennert County, died under unusual circumstances amid a plethora of rumors. Though the official cause of death was a heart attack, several rumors from that time suggested that the man was poisoned, or possibly even stabbed to death in a fit of rage. His wife, Victoria Imogene Llewelyn Crawford, who inherited the whole of Crawford's considerable fortune, was said to have grown tired of possible affairs with different women in the area, including, according to still more rumors of the time, one Angeline Blackbourne, who was the recipient of the land that became Crawford's Hollow back in the day.

Crawford, a socialite of the era, was well known for his financial support of several charities and his long-standing rivalry with other men in the area, though most of those rivalries seemed more in the nature of good-hearted competition than any actual conflicts. Upon his death Crawford was supposed to be buried in the family crypt, after spending a few days being viewed and remembered properly at the First Baptist Church of Wellman. Between the time of viewings and his scheduled burial, the body disappeared. The coffin Crawford's body rested in was not removed from the church. It was only his corpse which was apparently taken, or possibly got up and walked away.

At the time there were several rumors as to what might have happened, but no evidence was ever found of foul play, aside from the fact that his body simply vanished in the night.

Crowley sat at the table and sipped coffee while he looked over Thaddeus Crawford's journals. On one level there was little to see beyond the day-to-day existence of a businessman in the Civil War era. There were simple entries about who was seen, who was rumored to be in various scandals and who was not seen. It was moderately interesting, but hardly worth remembering half an hour later.

What made the journals interesting were the hidden pages. It took Crowley all of ten minutes to locate the pages that had been removed and stowed away inside the covers of the various journals, and then there were the pages that were written in code, where only certain keywords were actually part of the tale he needed to read.

Thaddeus Crawford was a very bad man. Born into a wealthy family, he very nearly quadrupled the family fortune in his lifetime, and made a point of claiming as much land as he possibly could in the name of the family fortune. He was fair in his dealings, mostly, but he was also hungry for more and more. Textiles, cotton, mining interests and more, Crawford had his hands in all of it.

Crawford's Hollow bore his name because at one point he owned the entire area. Though there was little mention of the property in his regular journals, the hidden affairs of his existence clarified that the property was traded to the Blackbournes in exchange for the sort of information the family could provide for him. They offered eldritch knowledge in exchange for the hollow: property for power, and Crowley would have been hard pressed to say who got the better end of that bargain without first studying the location carefully. He could sense the power there, even from a distance, but the exact type of power emanating from the Hollow would require intense studies he did not currently know if he had the time to consider. He made a note to check with Carter Decamp to see if he might have knowledge of the area.

It took little effort to discover that Crawford's body was taken shortly after his death, and that was a point of heavy interest. So, too, the knowledge that several of his peers died or vanished not long after Crawford himself. That knowledge did not come from the journals, of course, but by looking over the local newspapers and visiting the libraries at the local universities. Research, research, research, and then studying when it was time to change things up.

Twelve men, in total, vanished along with Crawford's corpse. The number was not likely to be a coincidence. More than one occult gathering found power in the number thirteen, a dark reflection of Christ and his twelve disciples.

A search of the fourth journal revealed an interesting note: *The deed is done. Ethan Crane has paid in full for what he did to little Melissa. Easy enough to hide her shame. In exchange for the bastard child and the land, the Blackbournes have introduced me to the wisdom of Nsnigoth, and shown me the way to powers I barely dared dream of before. Josiah Blackbourne and his sister, Angeline have been very accommodating, and while Melissa mourns the loss of her little one, she understands the shame she very nearly brought upon this family.*

Hiding Crane's body was easy enough, and using him as a sacrifice to Nsnigoth has opened gateways of perception and power that I never dreamed possible. I can feel the changes already taking place inside of me, and revel in them.

I fear the Blackbournes have outplayed me. I fear pleasures of the flesh may well have played a part in this, but I hold no anger toward the family. They gave me what I needed in exchange for land that was, frankly, of little mundane use, and while I suspect they have plans of their own, I do not foresee their efforts as counter to my own. They have their own agenda as we have our own agenda. I am a caterpillar and soon I will be a cocoon and after that I will emerge from my chrysalis a new and wondrous thing.

Crane is done. One less obstacle in my way. The last thorn in my side is Harrington, and I believe I know what must be done if I can only make myself do what is necessary. I have been a Christian man most of my life and it is challenging to break away from the careful indoctrination of a lifetime of rules, but, oh, it is also intoxicating.

Crowley looked at the notes and frowned. While there were easy connections to make, if one had the appropriate knowledge, some hints were vague enough to annoy him.

That was only one of the reasons he was glad to have Decamp along on this particular case. Carter had local knowledge that would likely prove invaluable.

More notes, and while he could connect the dots and understand that Crawford was part of a secret society, the notes were irritatingly vague on details as to where the society met and what their exact goals were. He could guess, of course. Nsnigoth was an Outer One, one of the so-called Entropic Gods, and one of those gods' many goals was simply chaos and transformation. Crawford wrote of the changes he was going through. He wrote of becoming something different. Like as not he expected godlike powers to be granted him somewhere down the line.

The skull-phantoms fed on eldritch energies according to what Decamp had discovered, but they also fed on the dead, and that was a problem because Don Washington's idiotic plans had worked too well. The dead did not rest in Wellman Georgia. Not right now, at least.

"Did you need more coffee?" The waitress looked like she'd last eaten sometime in the previous decade. She was skinny enough to nearly be gaunt, and her smile was tainted by the worst job of applying makeup he'd seen since the days when Tammy Faye Baker was constantly in the news.

Still, Crowley offered a quick smile and a thanks as she refilled his cup. The Waffle House was a dive, most twenty-four-hour diners were, but the coffee was passably good and he'd filled up on some concoction of chili and hash browns that was pleasantly tasty. The only other patrons were two men who were too drunk to consider driving anywhere, and one cop who was watching them to see if they would be stupid enough to try their luck. Crowley had no doubt that if they did, they'd be visiting the county lock up before the sun rose.

The final journal offered only one piece of hidden knowledge, an illustration concealed in the front cover, carefully folded over and slipped beneath the leather. The illustration was a simple diagram with exactly thirteen long shapes placed in a rough circle. Crawford had drawn crude stick figures of bodies lying on each of the rectangular shapes, and it was easy enough to understand that this was a plan for where thirteen bodies would be placed when the time was right. There was no date on the paper, but the paper was old and yellowed and the placement of the bodies was complex, a harsh geometric pattern laid out in a complex serpentine, all leading to one body set precisely in the center. Not a sacrifice. Crowley was sure of that. More likely where Crawford saw himself and his cohorts at the end of a dark ritual.

Whatever the case, the preparations likely had not worked out as planned. Crawford and his followers were amateurs, albeit imbued with certain knowledges, but the sort of rites he was likely to consider required decades of practice and knowledge, not mere months, or years, and from the notes he'd read and where they were placed. Crawford had not been active in his plan for more than a year or two before he disappeared.

Outside the clouds had finally dispersed, and the moon and stars lit the early morning skies, though the moon was on its descent and the sun would be up in a few hours. The air was cold, and Crowley was feeling his age.

He rose from his seat and placed the money for his meal along with a generous tip for a waitress who understood when her patron wanted to be left the hell alone.

Minutes later he was outside in the brisk night air. Not far away something watched him with eyes that glowed like candle flames, but whatever it was, it did not come closer, and it offered no threat. From what he could gather it was likely one of the Blackbourne clan. They might be dangerous but at the moment there was no reason to cause trouble.

Crowley blinked and yawned and when he looked again the night eyes had vanished as surely as a cat.

The night was full of dead things, but none were nearby, and Crowley was tired. A few hours' sleep then, long enough to recover from a wearying day.

Three a.m., the witching hour. It was a weeknight and most of Wellman had the good sense to be asleep. Mickie Conroy was not most people. She had big plans and those plans meant she had to be awake well after most of the world had gone to sleep.

There was a treasure hidden away in Wellman, Georgia, and she intended to find it. She intended to get rich, with no one the wiser.

There were endless rumors, of course, but she had it on good authority that the Blackbournes sometimes used a particular tree at the very edge of Crawford's Hollow as a drop point for meth or money. Stealing from that family was unwise, but Mickie was desperate. Her college tuition wasn't going to manifest. She was on the outs with her parents at the moment and they had no intention of paying for the next quarter. One little mistake and they expected her to come home and "get her act together."

Fuck that.

Mickie and her boyfriend were going to get that money together on their own. She knew she could pull her grades back up. She didn't need the drugs, not really; she didn't need to party. If she could prove that to her dad, and show him that she could get by without his help, then, knowing him, he'd offer to help again just to show how generous he was. She knew her logic would seem flawed to most people, but they didn't come from her family, or understand the way her dad's mind worked.

Jerry stumbled in the dark and almost fell on his face. He started giggling again and Mickie seriously considered beating his fool head in. They were currently at the Baptist church, where there was supposed to be another fortune hidden away. Why anyone would hide their money in a church was anyone's guess, but she didn't care. Between the two locations she hoped to find the money she needed and then some. If they found enough cash, it would be tuition and then a party or two. Jerry knew the score.

"You need to act right, Jerry. If we get busted here, it'll be serious." Not as serious as getting caught by the Blackbournes, which was why they were trying the church first. The Blackbournes were scary fuckers, and they were killers. Everyone knew it, even if no one did much about it as far as she was concerned. Jolene Blackbourne was just a bitch, but Lament Blackbourne? There were stories about what the woman did to her enemies and they were grim tales at best.

Jerry giggled. "Calm down, babe. No one's gonna come by this time of night."

He tried groping her and got his hand slapped. There'd be time for that later.

There was a rustling sound nearby, like a flag fluttering in a strong breeze, and before Mickie could do more than turn her head, she saw the things coming their way. There were three of the shapes. Hooded apparitions that dropped from the skies and held out cadaverous, clawed hands.

Jerry let out a squawk of surprise and tripped over his own feet as one of the things reached for him. It missed him. The second one in line did better, yanking the necklace from around his neck, a small figure he'd gotten from his grandmother, that was supposed to be his good luck charm. Whatever the case, the creature yanked hard at the leather strap around his neck, fingers cutting into his throat even as the thing captured the creepy ass good luck charm he always wore.

Jerry's eyes rolled back in his head. The totem he wore—which was a little figure of what seemed like a man made from snakes as far as she could ever tell—crumbled and something happened to the thing holding that trinket. For a moment it seemed more vital, more alive, and then the totem withered like a flower rotting away. One moment it was whole and the next the necklace's centerpiece simply crumbled into dust.

Jerry seized. His mouth hung open, and his entire body twitched and then thrashed violently as the hand of the thing tore something out of him. The bony fingers reached into his chest without seeming to cause any wounds, and then yanked back and took something from Jerry that had him falling down without another movement on his part.

She knew in that instant that Jerry was dead. Sweet Jerry, who was a stoner, yes, but also a genuinely good person. He listened when she was having problems, he held her when she cried, and he promised to help her get the money she needed, knowing the risks. And he was gone, snuffed out in an instant.

Mickie screamed. Her heart felt rimed in ice, and her stomach was even worse, because something killed Jerry and she didn't want to believe that was possible.

She turned and started running, not looking before she was on the move, trying to get away from the dark shapes now looking in her direction.

She made two steps before she saw the fourth shape.

It was not the same, but it was similar. There was a dark cloak long enough to drag the ground, and there was a hood, and inside that hood she could only see darkness but there was shape to the darkness, a definite shadow inside the hood that looked toward her with hungry, glittering malevolence.

Two more steps before she could stop her forward motion and try to, please God, change her course.

She was too late. The hands reached out for her, stretched in her direction and caught her shoulders.

It did not speak but Mickie let loose another wail of terror as the thing pulled her closer. Her screams died off as she felt her very soul torn from her body.

Perhaps she should have felt honored if she knew that it was Thaddeus Crawford himself who stole her life away. Finally after so very long, he felt himself evolving, becoming something else. Something magnificent.

He did not speak. He did not need to. Energies flowed to him from his followers, rippling through his body as they came to him.

He was becoming.

In the darkness of the early morning, Thaddeus Crawford looked around and felt a powerful satisfaction. He was so very hungry, ravenous, but he knew that he would be feasting soon, and the meal would be never ending.

In the darkness his followers gathered for one moment to look at him and revel in the presence of their new lord.

The veil between the worlds was thin in Wellman, and growing thinner by the day, by the hour, and Crawford looked at that veil knowing that soon he would be able to tear it asunder.

He had spent years, decades contemplating the rituals, communing with the god he had chosen, that had chosen him. Nsnigoth, called the Devourer, the Reaver and a thousand other titles.

The thing that had been Thaddeus Crawford looked at the dead bodies before him and focused his will. As with the necklace a few moments earlier the bodies lost their cohesion and crumbled into dust, leaving behind a few small pieces of metal, braces from the man child and fillings and earrings from the woman child. In minutes the rest of the remains blew away in the autumn winds.

Still he did not speak. He had nothing to say just yet, but soon, very soon he would sing to his god, a song of destruction and rebirth.

Until then his servants would feed, and serve him well.

Sascha showed up at the Strand house a little before noon. She had obviously taken the time to stop at home and get cleaned up. Her hair was pinned back. Her makeup was freshly applied and more subtle than usual. Travis had always thought of her as one of the most "together" people he had ever met, but the events of the last few days had shown him Sascha was just as vulnerable as anyone. She had lost that air of complete confidence he had normally associated with her.

Travis and Emily resumed their seats on the couch (though not as close together) and Sascha took a chair facing them. Travis said, "How did things go with the sheriff?"

Sascha said, "Just as your Mr. Decamp said they would. We told Sheriff Price the version of the story Decamp advised. Don arrived before us and we found him…as he was. The sheriff took our statements and told us we could go. He said he would want to talk to us again later. There was no mention of Decamp's call."

"Decamp was here earlier," Travis said. He related the events of the morning and what Cindy Kane had said.

"God," Sascha said. "Won't this ever be over?"

Emily said, "Carter is working on it. He and his friend Mr. Crowley have some ideas about what's actually going on."

Sascha spread her hands. "And we're just supposed to sit here and wait?"

Travis said, "I don't really see what else we can do, Sascha. Oh, is Mark okay? Is he coming over?"

Sascha shook her head. "I think seeing what happened to Don affected Mark pretty badly. He went straight home after we left the farm, and I haven't heard from him since."

"We'll check on him later today," Emily said. "I don't blame him for freaking out. I'm amazed you're holding up as well as you are, Sascha."

Sascha said, "Don't be too impressed. I'm just barely holding it together. All these years of studying the paranormal, and then to see something like what happened last night."

Travis heard the muffled groan of the central heat kicking on. The day had turned cool and overcast and the clouds had a look of coming rain.

Travis said, "Decamp said Jonathan Crowley was going to get Thaddeus Crawford's journals from Mark's house. Maybe that will give them some useful information."

Sascha said, "I have a file on Crawford. He's never really figured in any of my studies, but just the fact that he used to own Crawford's Hollow made me interested in him. Weird things have been happening there for decades."

Emily said, "There was something mysterious about his death too, wasn't there?"

Sascha said, "His body disappeared not long after his death. It's all kind of muddled. I'll get my file and give it a look. There might be something in there of use."

"I'm sure Decamp would like to have a look at it," Travis said.

Sascha looked at him for a moment. "You certainly seem to have a lot of faith in Carter Decamp. You just met him."

Emily said, "There's something about him that inspires confidence. It's hard to explain."

Travis said, "And you know that thing that flew down and attacked the scarecrow? He killed one of them right in front of me."

Sascha said, "That's impressive, I'll admit. Maybe he *can* help us."

Emily said, "At this point, I'm counting on it."

Sascha said, "Okay. How about this. I'm going to go home and dig into my files. Why don't you two come by in a couple of hours, maybe after you check on Mark. We'll go over what we know and what's happened since and see if we can come up with anything we can do."

Travis was glad to see a little of Sascha's spirit returning. He'd hated seeing her so subdued. "I think that's a really good idea. I don't like sitting around doing nothing any more than you do. Especially after what happened to Don."

Sascha said, "Yes. He wasn't my favorite person, but he was one of us."

"Nsnigoth," Carter Decamp said. He said it quietly, but to Cindy Kane it seemed the word had a sibilant echo. "That would explain much."

"Who or what is Nsnigoth?" Cindy said.

Jonathan Crowley said, "One of the outer ones. An ancient god. Old and bloody and dark."

They were sitting in Crowley's room in a motel just outside Wellman city limits. Decamp and Crowley were in chairs on either side of the room's small table, and Cindy sat on one corner of the bed. A stack of old journals rested on the tabletop.

Cindy said, "I've heard Dad mention the Dark Gods. Any connection?"

Crowley said, "Different pantheon but similar in that both represent extra-dimensional entities with scores to settle."

Decamp said, "Nsnigoth, also known as the devourer. Usually considered the most powerful of the Outer Ones. His brethren include Zdrey, Mekelar, and Heng. They are sometimes called primal gods or entropic gods, but the latter term is the more appropriate. They are entities that thrive on chaos, pain, and suffering."

"And people worship these things?" Cindy said.

"Not many anymore," Decamp said. "Once there were temples to them across the ancient world. Thousands of years ago, before the great cataclysm, the Outer Ones wielded considerable power."

"What happened to them?"

Decamp smiled. "That is a long story and best kept for another time, my dear. The short version is they, along with other extra-dimensional beings, were shunted off this plane of reality. What power they exert in our world now is through influencing human followers."

Cindy said, "And you think Crawford was one of those followers. What would he get out of it?"

Crowley said, "Power. The Outer Ones grant boons to their worshipers, sometimes in the form of material wealth, and sometimes as actual eldritch power. In the most extreme cases, the servants of the entropic gods become almost demigods themselves. The Soul Eater of Mesopotamia. The Dollmaker. The Queen of Flies and the Flayed Man. We call these aberrations Outer Lords."

"Whoa," Cindy said. "You think that was Crawford's goal?"

"I think it very possible," said Decamp. "Remember what we discussed about Wellman being a liminal area. Not too long ago a local funeral parlor owner named Henry Thayer tried to do that very thing. He was collecting souls and offering them to Nsnigoth in hopes of becoming an Outer Lord. Fortunately, Carl Price and Wade Griffin stopped him."

"I can believe that," Cindy said. Her own experience with Griffin and Price had shown her they were men to be reckoned with. She'd seen them face down drug dealers and demons alike.

Crowley said, "But it looks like somebody killed him before he could complete his plan. You're the expert on the history of the area, Carter. What do you think happened?"

Decamp said, "There are many rumors about Crawford's death, but once I knew what I was looking for, I was able to locate the report from the coroner's inquest from 1872."

"Of course you were," said Cindy.

"The attending physician," Decamp continued, "a man named Jennings, listed the official cause of death as a heart attack. But in his report, Jennings said the heart was damaged 'as if the fist of God had closed around it,' which is suggestive."

Crowley said, "You're thinking the Blackbourne family."

"I'm not following you," Cindy said.

Decamp said, "You may recall, my dear, I told you the Blackbournes are the descendants of a race of inter-dimensional beings. The less-human members of the family actually live in several dimensions at once. Such a being can pass physical barriers in our world by shifting slightly into another dimension. I've seen them do it. One of them could reach into someone's chest and crush his heart but leave no marks on the body."

Cindy said, "Crawford said in one of his journals he thought the Blackbournes might have outwitted him somehow."

Decamp nodded. "He sold them Crawford's Hollow for a pittance, thinking it worthless land. He didn't know that the hollow was a perfect spot for an inter-dimensional nexus. The Blackbournes had long range plans for the area. In exchange they gave Crawford knowledge of the Outer Ones and their ancient sorcery."

"But why would they kill him later?" Cindy said.

Decamp said, "Loathe as I am to speculate, there we enter the grounds of conjecture. I suspect the Blackbournes didn't think Crawford would be able to make much use of the information they gave him. But he turned out to be more adept than they thought, and not only succeeded in contacting Nsnigoth, but actually managed to gain power from the Outer Ones. At that point they would have considered him a threat and dealt with him accordingly."

Cindy said, "Nice family, these Blackbournes."

Crowley said, "Since we know what Crawford did to Harrington, it's likely he had used a considerable amount of his newly found power to work that bit of revenge. The Blackbournes caught him at a low ebb and snuffed him out."

"My thinking exactly, Jonathan," Decamp said. "Crawford was killed just when he was about to attain his goals."

"Somebody like that would have had a contingency plan," Crowley said. "Which brings us to this bit of cryptic artwork."

Crowley spread a weathered yellow sheet of paper on the table and Cindy leaned closer to see it. It was a diagram of some sort, showing twelve rectangles arrayed in a rough circle around another rectangle. All the shapes had stick figures drawn on them.

Decamp put a finger on the center rectangle and said, "Crawford had plans for himself and all his followers in the event of his untimely demise."

Crowley said, "I'm betting the other members of his cult spirited him away and put him in some secret room. After their own deaths, they would have joined him there."

Decamp said, "Yes, we know the cult they belonged to was active at least into the 1920s. A man named Thomas Burke was said to have meetings with robed figures in his house and the surrounding woods."

Cindy said, "But what good would that do Crawford? He was dead, wasn't he?"

Crowley said, "There's dead and then there's dead. Crawford's spirit was already corrupted by the Outer Ones. It may have simply gone dormant."

"Dormant and waiting," said Decamp.

"We need to find those bodies, Carter," Crowley said. "Tomorrow night is Halloween and that doesn't bode well. All of this spirit activity has been building toward something. Finding Crawford's mortal remains might allow us to stop whatever's coming."

Decamp said, "The chamber shown in that diagram would have to be quite large. There weren't that many places someone could have built something like that in the 1870s. We should probably take another look through the journals and see what we can glean."

Cindy said, "There's a faster way, Carter. You could let me hold one of the journals. I could probably use it to find Crawford."

Decamp looked over at her. "I don't think that's a good idea, my dear. Crawford isn't someone you need to invite contact with."

"I helped you find a demon. I'm willing to do this. My head's been screwed up since this started."

Crowley said, "Psychometry?"

Cindy nodded. "It's my primary talent."

Crowley said, "Decamp has a point. Given Crawford's association with the Outer Ones, if you become aware of him, he might be able to sense you as well."

Cindy said, "Then you and Carter will just have to protect me. It's not like I haven't already been singled out in all of this. My phantom pains and the other things I've felt since touching Harrington's grave. I feel like I've been running scared and I don't like that feeling. I want to do this. Let me try."

Decamp said, "All right, Cindy. But let me take certain precautions first."

Cindy smiled. "I'd expect no less."

———

Sheriff Carl Price was already at the bar in McGarity's Tavern when Dave Braxton arrived. Price sat at the far corner of the bar where he could see the whole room. He nodded at Braxton as he entered.

Braxton hadn't seen Price in a couple of months. He looked about the same as ever. A big man with broad shoulders and close-cropped hair. His nose had been broken at least once. Braxton had always liked Price. People expected rivalry between police and sheriff's departments, but he and Price had always cooperated with one another.

"Carl," Braxton said when he reached the bar.

"Dave," said Price. "Thanks for meeting me. I have a little info for you. The kind best kept off the phone."

Braxton said, "So you mentioned."

The bartender, a young Latina woman with blue hair and a nose ring came over to the two men. "What are you drinking?"

Braxton pointed at Price. "What's he drinking?"

"House beer. It's all he ever drinks here."

"Give me that."

"Cops," Blue Hair said, but she smiled when she said it. She turned and went to get Braxton's order.

Braxton turned back to Price. "What have you got?"

"I got an anonymous tip last night to come out to the Harper farm. I went to check on it and found a dead guy mostly sunk into the ground. Just his head sticking up."

"Jesus. I haven't heard about it yet," said Braxton.

"I was keeping it quiet until I could talk to you. Dead guy's name was Don Washington. Not a local. Student over at Gatesville U."

The bartender came back with Braxton's beer and put it on the counter. She gave him a grin and wandered off to help another customer.

"She likes you," Price said.

Braxton said, "Looks like it. So what happened?"

"Like I said, I got a call and drove out. There were two other kids there. They told me they were part of a group of paranormal investigators, and they'd been looking into some weird stuff around Wellman. They were supposed to meet their friend, the Washington kid, at the farm. When they got there, they found him like I did."

Braxton said, "Buried in the ground."

"That's just it. He wasn't exactly buried. There was no sign of digging. No loose earth. It was like the ground had turned into quicksand and he had been sucked down into it. Then it closed around him."

"That's crazy," said Braxton.

"It gets worse. I had some deputies come up to dig him out for the M.E. They had a hell of a time getting him out of the ground because he was all wrapped up in vines. And get this. The vines were rooted. Like they had grown around Washington."

"What the hell, Carl. What did the other kids say?"

"Not much. Just stuck to their story. They came to meet him and found him that way."

"You believe them?"

"More or less. They sure as hell couldn't have put him in the ground like that. Hell, even if he had been buried, whoever did it would have needed a front-end loader or something. You couldn't dig a narrow hole like that with shovels."

Braxton shook his head. "Fucking Wellman."

"Yeah," said Price. "Anyway, scuttlebutt is you've had a couple of weird incidents yourself."

"What have you heard?"

"Something about a statue at the Methodist church," said Price.

"Roger that. Much like your guy in the ground, I have a situation I can't explain." Braxton gave Carl a short version of the events around the statue and what the physical evidence suggested. He added what he knew about the gruesome killing at the Wellman House Museum too.

Price said, "Like you said, fucking Wellman."

Braxton said, "I don't guess Ron Pang has any ideas yet?"

"I doubt he's even had a chance to look at the body yet. It was pretty early this morning when we brought it in."

Braxton said, "So both branches of law enforcement in the area have unsolved murders with crazy-ass physical evidence. What the hell do we do now?"

Price took a long swig of his beer. "Wait and see, I guess. I've been here before, Dave. You know my father was sheriff back in the day. He told me some stories about weird stuff that happened in Wellman that was never resolved."

Braxton said, "You know what the weirdest part of all this is to me?"

"There's a weirdest part?" said Price.

"Yeah. It's not just the that the physical evidence we have doesn't make sense. It's the lack of the usual types of evidence. No fingerprints. Nothing on surveillance cameras. In the museum case there wasn't any blood spatter. Like the guy had been chopped up and then dropped into the basement. I'll tell you, Carl, it's almost enough to make a man believe in ghosts."

"Ain't it just," said Price.

Mark Irvin lived in a small apartment complex located north of Wellman, just off Highway 5. Travis pulled into an open space in front of the building around noon. Emily tried Mark's number on her phone for the third time. He hadn't responded to calls or texts all morning.

"Maybe he's asleep," Emily said. "He was out really late."

Travis said, "Maybe. I want to check, just to be sure. With so many weird things going on, I don't want to take anything for granted."

Mark's car was in its usual slot, and Travis took that as a good sign. He and Emily climbed out of the Toyota. The afternoon had turned blustery, and leaves rained from a big oak tree near one side of Mark's building. Mark was on the ground floor, apartment number 118.

Travis knocked on the door. He glanced over at Emily, who was staring at the door as if willing it to open. Travis had long known she had a thing for Mark. He wondered if recent events had changed that in any way.

After waiting several minutes, Travis knocked again, louder this time. "Mark, It's Travis. Open up, man. I want to be sure you're all right."

Travis thought he heard movement inside the apartment and then he heard the lock turn. The door swung inward a few inches and Mark looked out at him. "I'm okay, Travis. I just don't want to talk to anyone right now."

Emily said, "Can we come in, Mark? We're worried about you."

Mark said, "Sorry, but no. I want to think all of this through, and I want to do it alone. I can tell you this much. I'm done. I don't want anything more to do with all this. No more ghost hunting."

Travis said, "I know how you feel, man, but you shouldn't try to go this alone. And I don't think any of us can just walk away at this point."

Mark said, "I'm sure as hell going to try. Thanks for coming to check on me. I'll call you later."

Mark closed the door. Emily looked over at Travis and he shrugged. Together they turned and walked back toward the car.

"I'm feeling really helpless," Emily said.

"Me too, but what can we do? We can't make him come with us."

"You don't think he'd…"

"Kill himself?" Travis said. "I thought of that too, but no, I don't think he would. He's just overwhelmed by all this. I don't blame him."

Emily said, "Me either. Maybe we can try again in a day or so."

Travis said, "We'll see what Sascha thinks. She knows him better than I do."

Half an hour later, Travis and Emily pulled up in front of the Wurdilec house. It was a big, boxy building, all concrete and glass. Sascha liked to joke it had been designed by Frank Lloyd Wrong. Whoever had designed it, it had cost a lot of money.

Sascha stepped out onto the front steps as Travis and Emily got out of the car. She waved as they came up the concrete walk. "Mom and Dad are away, so we have the place to ourselves."

"Probably a good thing," said Emily.

Sascha ushered them in, then led them through a massive living room into an equally massive dining room. The long dining table was piled high with books and papers. Sascha's laptop sat on one corner.

Sascha said, "Did you talk to Mark?"

Travis said, "We stopped by his place and saw him for just a minute. He didn't want to talk to us or anyone else right now."

"I guess we can't blame him. I would have liked to talk to him about Thaddeus Crawford's journals, but we'll just have to do without them for now."

Emily said, "So what just *are* we going to do?"

Sascha said, "I've been thinking since we talked this morning. Looking for something to help us take some sort of action. Then I thought of the one thing we have that no one else does." She pointed at the stacks of papers. "We have the *Tourist's Guide to Haunted Wellman*. Or at least the manuscript."

"How does that help us?" Travis said.

Sascha slid into a chair and motioned for the others to be seated. "This whole thing is about the folklore of the area. The urban legends and ghost stories related to Wellman. That's how this started. Whatever Don did, he set these things loose."

"And we watched him," said Travis.

Sascha nodded. "Yes, we're far from blameless in this. But we have to move forward. I've pulled anything in the manuscript and notes having to do with Crawford and his circle and read back through it. I think I may have found something. Do you remember the chapter about Ethan Crane and the First Baptist Church?"

Travis said, "Yeah, that was one of the creepier things we ran across. No one ever knew why his body was found inside the church wall or who had killed him."

"You may remember the church was rebuilt several times. The last time in 1878, ostensibly because the congregation had grown too large."

"Ostensibly?" said Emily.

Sascha said, "I found out that the population records don't support that. The congregation couldn't have grown too big at that time because the population of Wellman didn't increase that much."

"Maybe they were looking toward the future," Emily said. "Or someone made a big donation."

Sascha said, "Possibly, but I'm just going with the facts I have. It doesn't matter that much because noticing that was what made me look at these." She put two large, rolled up sheets of paper on the table. "These are the floor plans of the 1878 version of the church and the one it replaced."

Travis unrolled one of the sheets and looked at it. "Where did you get these?"

Sascha said, "I've had them. They came with a bunch of county records I acquired when we first started working on the books. I just hadn't had much reason to look at them. It gets more interesting."

Sascha pulled her laptop over and opened it. Travis and Emily moved to where they could see the screen.

Sascha said, "These are both architectural drawings, so they're to scale. I scanned them and put the images one on top of the other. Look here. The major portion of the 1878 rebuild is built almost to one side of the previous building. The new foundation overlaps the old, but only by a little. They practically dug a new foundation. That hadn't been the case in the previous rebuilds."

"Maybe the old one had grown unstable," Travis said. "The place was hit with cannon fire during the Civil War."

"Again, I'm not speculating. Just going with available facts. What I'm thinking is the old foundation was covered over, leaving a big underground room just off the side of the new church."

Emily said, "Why would anyone do that?"

"Maybe someone needed the space for things they didn't want the good citizens of Wellman to be aware of. If the church really didn't need to be rebuilt but it was done anyway, it suggests something odd was going on." Sascha reached for another sheet of paper. "And this is the clincher. Part of the bill for supplies and labor for the new church. Guess who paid for it."

"Thaddeus Crawford," Emily said.

"None other," said Sascha.

Travis said, "Jeez, Sascha. That's some good detective work."

Sascha said, "Thank you. I'm pretty proud of myself."

Travis said, "Okay, so say there's a big underground room under the Baptist church. What's in there?"

Sascha said, "I don't know for certain, but I suspect it may be where Crawford's body is hidden. In any case, I want to have a look. I think we should go to the church tonight."

Emily said, "Break into a church?"

Travis grinned. "We won't have to break in. Wellman still has a lot of small-town sensibilities. They don't lock the church doors, even now. But I think they do have services tonight."

Sascha said, "We'll be going long after services are over. Let's plan on meeting there about one tomorrow morning."

Travis said, "We should probably let Decamp know what we're doing. The skull-phantoms are still out there."

"I'd rather we didn't," Sascha said. "We started this and I think we should finish it."

Travis said, "I'd rather not finish it by getting killed, Sascha."

"I could be completely wrong about this. They may have just filled the old foundation in with rubble or as you said, it may have become unusable. Let's just go and have a look at the place before we bring anyone else in."

Travis sighed. "Okay. We'll have a look. But I still don't think it's a good idea."

"Turn left here," Cindy said.

Carter Decamp did as she said. They were in his BMW, with Cindy riding shotgun and Jonathan Crowley in the back seat. They had been driving around for about half an hour since leaving Crowley's motel a little after midnight.

Cindy held one of Crawford's journals, the one in which the chamber sketches had been hidden. She had expected another psychic bombardment when she had touched it, but so far she felt only a faint pull. Maybe Crawford hadn't noticed her yet. With any luck he wouldn't until they found him. After that it was Crowley and Carter's problem.

The streets of downtown Wellman were mostly deserted. They would certainly be full on the following evening, Halloween. Right now, the town's macabre holiday decorations looked more sinister than usual as an errant wind swirled down the main street, tugging at the garments of pumpkin-headed manikins, and sending orange and black streamers aflutter. The rain slicked asphalt threw back dull reflections from storefront windows, streetlights, and traffic signals. Welcome autumn, Cindy thought. Bring your cheer.

"Left again," Cindy said.

"We're heading toward the Baptist church," Decamp said.

Crowley said, "One of our top contenders for Crawford's hidden chamber."

"You guys sure you needed me?" Cindy said.

"Very much so," said Decamp. "I had at least half a dozen possible locations for Crawford's hiding place. You're saving valuable time, my dear. I appreciate the risk you're taking."

Crowley said, "What Carter said. But when we do find Crawford, you're out of this, Cindy. I've seen what malevolent entities can do to psychic sensitives."

Cindy said, "You can count on that, Mr. Crowley. The last time I stayed too close to the action, some demons came after me."

"You'll have to tell me about that," Crowley said. "And call me Jonathan."

Cindy held up one hand. "Ow. We're close. Very close."

"The church is just ahead," said Decamp.

"Lock and load," said Crowley. "Figuratively speaking."

Decamp stopped a block away from the church and pulled the sedan up to a curb. He and Crowley got out of the car. Decamp hefted his walking stick. Cindy stepped out as well and walked around to the driver's side.

"Get well away from here, my dear," Decamp said, handing her his keys. "I'll call you when this is over."

Cindy said, "Please don't get killed. Either of you."

Crowley smiled. "We'll do our best. It's been good enough so far."

Cindy watched as the two men started walking toward the church. Then she got into the BMW, wheeled it around, and drove away from whatever was coming.

———

The most recent version of the First Baptist Church of Wellman had stood for over 150 years, but it had received several facelifts in that time. Still, under the red brick façade that had been added in the 1960s, one could still see the basic Gothic shape of the original in the domed windows and doors. The front steps were marble, cut from local quarries, and stained glass set in the windows had been imported from England.

Travis had always found the place a little creepy. His parents hadn't been much for religion, but he had visited the place several times with friends and relatives. Sascha parked her car off to one side of the main building so as not to be easily visible from the street.

The old building loomed in bright moonlight under dark scudding clouds. A front was pushing through and the wind blew cold and dry, displacing the moisture from earlier in the day and scattering leaves before it.

"I really don't want to go in there," Emily said as they got out of the car.

Travis said, "You can wait out here if you want. I'll go in with Sascha."

Emily said, "I want to wait out here alone even less than I want to go in. let's just get this over with."

The trio looked left and right as they rounded a corner to the front of the building, making sure no late-night drivers were passing by. Then they hurried up the steps and stepped through the front doors. It was dark inside the foyer. As black as a witch's heart, as Travis's grandmother used to say.

Travis produced a small flashlight and shined the beam on the floor. He intended to keep the beam pointed downwards and not at any of the windows. All they needed was a passing patrol car to see a light moving around inside the church.

Sascha said, "We need to cross to the far side of the sanctuary and go down to basement." Her voice sounded too loud in the silence within.

Travis nodded and together the three of them went into the sanctuary and hurried down the center aisle. They barely needed the flashlight because moonlight was streaming through the tall narrow windows. The lead dividers between the panes of stained glass made an odd pattern on the floor. The empty pews gave the place a haunted look.

They passed the pulpit and went through a door at the rear of the sanctuary. Just inside the doorway, a stairwell yawned, and narrow steps went down into darkness.

What exactly does a ghost look like? Is it different from a specter? A wraith? A poltergeist?

In many cases the witnesses of spectral activity claim that the restless dead look identical to the living, or that they are semi-transparent, but otherwise look the same. Sometimes the eyewitnesses claim they look as they did at the moment of death, bloodied or wounded and carrying those marks for all eternity.

In literary works the dead range from invisible, to ghastly apparitions, to figures wrapped in shrouds and tied with the chains they forged in life, anchored in place by regrets and a lifetime of sins.

The true answer is anyone's guess. Eyewitness reports are as varied as the people who make them. Each ghost seems to follow their own rules, and the rules are never quite the same.

In the case of certain Civil War ghosts they appear as they did in life, unchanging for eternity, and in the case of the ghost of Abbey Road, often reported though no history of why a ghost manifests is known, it is a headless Union soldier that several people have witnessed.

Perhaps the strangest of ghosts are indeed the ones wrapped in funeral shrouds, the white sheets seen floating in the air, who might well be a prankster trying to scare the locals, if indeed there were legs or feet to see under those sheets.

A dozen different eyewitnesses have reported seeing some of the ghosts mentioned here in The Tourist's Guide To Haunted Wellman, *often with completely different reports as to exactly what they have witnessed.*

Perhaps, just maybe, the differing reports are a sign that the ghosts are being falsely reported. Just as likely, however, the truth is a little different. Just as a dozen different witnesses can see the same person rob a bank and offer different descriptions to a police sketch artist, maybe the witnesses all see the same apparition and simply perceive the dead with differing eyes to detail.

Maybe the ghosts can decide how they look, or maybe their ectoplasmic residues resonate differently for every eyewitness.

"Going by the plans, the hidden part of the foundation should be behind that wall," Sascha said, pointing to one side of the basement room.

Travis shined the flashlight beam across a wall of unpainted drywall. Mold made patterns on the wall only some mad god could read. He didn't see any side of the door, but then he hadn't expected to. It wouldn't be a hidden room if there was an obvious entrance.

Sascha stepped up to the drywall and began rapping on it with her knuckles. She walked the length of the wall, then came back to a certain spot and rapped again.

"Here," Sascha said. "The door is here. It must have been covered over when the last of Crawford's acolytes were brought here. It's not like ghosts would need a door."

Emily said, "How do we get in?"

"With any luck it's just an empty doorway behind the drywall," said Sascha. "We need something to break through."

Travis played the light around the room. It fell on a two by four leaning against the wall. He handed the light to Sascha and picked up the board. He crossed the room and swung his new cudgel into the drywall. The tip plunged through with a hollow "pop." Travis struck the spot twice more and the old drywall fell inward. A gaping hole yawned at them.

Travis turned to take back his light, but Sascha stepped past him and into the hole. He looked over at Emily and shook his head before following. He found himself in a room so large the far walls were invisible in the feeble light.

The darkness was nearly complete, as deep and rich as night could be, and the room held secrets best not contemplated by sane individuals. A bunch of big stone slaps lay carefully placed at odd angles to each other, seemingly in a state of disarray. On each table lay what remained of a human body.

Travis sensed somehow the placement was not a random thing. It felt like there was an order to where each table had been placed with their bizarre burdens. Since Sascha still had his flashlight and they were well out of range of prying eyes from outside the church, Travis pulled out his phone and switched its light on.

He counted the slabs. Thirteen tables, thirteen corpses. The bodies were wrapped in moldering cloth, each cadaver set in different positions in the darkness. Like as not they'd been settled in the same way once upon a time, the arms crossed over the chest, the face pointed toward the dark ceiling above them, but that had changed over time. The corpses were mummified. Dry air and time had drawn the moisture from flesh and left bones wrapped in leathery skin, the limbs drawn into the body as tendons shriveled and muscles atrophied. The shrouds over each body stained by time and darker things.

Now the bodies were shifted into different positions, limbs tucked in close to the bodies, pulled tight as decay took a gradual toll.

How long had they sat undisturbed? Very nearly a century had gone by. No. Travis shook his head. Longer than that. Well over a hundred years and to one had set foot in the tomb where thirteen men lay silent in their graves, even if the spirits of the dead were far noisier.

These were the skull-phantoms?

These shrouded collections of dried meat and bones?

They should have been dust, near as he could figure, but something, some force, had mummified them instead of letting them rot away. He could smell a collection of spices in the air, a faint aroma of cinnamon and other essences. Maybe the dead here had been mummified properly. He had no way of knowing and no intention of cutting into the bodies to find out in any event. He had no idea why they still existed, but each and every corpse was intact instead of being little more than powder left on tables.

Some of them lay on their sides, broken as a child's pinata, with crushed limbs or in one case a severed head. The caul of dust around those forms was disturbed in strange ways as if they'd fought across the marble tables. Others were completely intact, and at the epicenter of the collected tables, what he expected was the corpse of Thaddeus Crawford was in a sitting position, the withered remains pulled into the very center of the marble slab, both legs under the corpse in a modified lotus posture, hands resting on knees, the head lowered as if in contemplation.

He stared at the bodies and shook his head as the light from his phone carved away slices of the darkness to reveal one form after another.

Emily whispered as if she were in a sacred place. Perhaps she was, in some people's eyes. She said, "It's bigger than I thought it would be." Despite her near silence, the words echoed across the chamber and bounced from elaborately painted walls. There were words carved on the walls in a language none of them recognized, and scenes from some ancient time depicted a dark shape looming over ancient pyramids of a sort that almost looked like they belonged to the Aztecs. Armies fled from the vast darkness, or bowed in supplication in at least one of the paintings. Whatever the case, that dark form was gigantic in comparison.

"Is that supposed to be Nsnigoth?" Emily spoke again and the beam from her phone illuminated one of the paintings where the vast darkness rose over an army of the suffering. Travis shrugged, for the moment incapable of speaking. His mouth was too dry. His eyes were wide in his head and his pulse seemed loud enough to deafen him.

He wanted to step closer to the nearest mummified remains, but his feet did not move, seemed incapable of rising from the marble floor of the tomb, as if he'd taken root.

Sascha slipped past him effortlessly, the borrowed flashlight focused on the sitting remains of Thaddeus Crawford. Heavy cobwebs draped the funeral shroud, showing it had not been moved in a very long time. Travis stared on as she slowly circled the corpse on its pedestal. For the first time he saw that a mask of some sort covered the mummy's face. Whatever the design of that mask, it was submerged in shadows, hidden by the dark, rotting cloth of the body's funeral shroud. Dark holes were lost in shadows where the eyes should have been, but still he felt like the corpse was staring at him.

"We should call Carter Decamp." Emily's voice seemed a little stronger now.

"Not yet," Sascha said. "Soon, but we need to see this. We need to know what we're looking at and to understand it."

"Why?"

Sascha turned her head and stared at her friend, seemingly surprised by the question. "Because we've earned this, Emily. We found this first, and this is exactly what we've been trying to understand." Both of the women spoke softly, but they no longer whispered. Travis said nothing, not trusting his voice not to shake, or that he would make any point clearly enough. He felt like he was swimming through a fog as he looked around.

A rustling noise caught his attention, and Travis's eyes focused on the corpse of Thaddeus Crawford, which seemed the source of that strange sound.

Madness, of course. Corpses did not move.

Except.

The caul of cobwebs around the head of the corpse drifted on a negligible breeze, sheared away from the main mass of the cobweb covering the remains. Damned if the head didn't look like it had turned to face Sascha as she stood in front of the corpse.

"Sascha…" His voice was a squeak, too dry by far.

Sascha backpedaled away from the table, her hip running into the edge of the next closest pedestal.

"Did he move?" Sascha's voice was far too loud and shook.

Travis couldn't convince his tongue to peel away from the roof of his mouth, and so he nodded his answer. Sascha retreated another few paces, her hip sliding along the marble slab where the broken remains of one of Crawford's followers lay wasting away in near complete darkness.

"We need to go. Now." Emily's voice brooked no argument. She was looking at her phone and ready to start dialing. "I'm calling Carter." Her voice shook and she looked round with wide, wild eyes. "I mean it."

Travis nodded in the darkness, and Sascha said, "Call him," in a very small voice.

The shroud around the withered remains of Thaddeus Crawford rustled in the still air, and this time Travis saw the head as it turned toward Sascha's voice.

"Run!"

Sascha ran track. She bolted past him without saying a word, her pretty face pulled into a mask of fear.

He was right behind her, his arm reaching to pull Emily along for the ride, just in case she had ideas of calling Decamp from inside the dark room. He needn't have bothered. She moved on her own and while it wasn't a full tilt run, it was close.

Something disturbed their mortal remains.

They were no longer tied to the tomb where their bodies lay. They were beyond that now, or so they believed, but every last one of them felt it when the air blew across their mummified remains, and maybe they were mistaken. Though Nsnigoth had blessed them with transformation, none of them understood the workings of the god, or dared question what had been done to them in order to allow their continued existence.

Not even Thaddeus Crawford, or what had been Crawford in life.

The air in their tomb was disturbed, and like moths drawn to a powerful light in the darkness, they felt a compulsion to examine what was happening. They moved from all over the area, leaving behind the prey they'd been stalking and preparing to torment and destroy.

On Hardscrabble Road a man named Keith Vintner clutched at his chest in the throes of a heart attack brought on by fear. The skull-phantom released him from its grip and rose into the air, and Vintner, unaware that he'd even been haunted, slid down in a daze. He never awakened again. His heart stopped minutes later.

On Highway 41 Lizzie Monterey did her best to comfort her newborn daughter, Sandra, who fidgeted and cried enough to wake the dead. Lizzie could not see the specter feasting on Sandra's soul, but her daughter stopped crying as the creature went its own way, leaving the infant traumatized but alive. The only lasting result was a phobia that would grow over time. Sandra's fear of death was a palpable thing from that day forward.

The servants of Thaddeus Crawford came together, a gathering of darkness large enough to create a cold spot in the skies above the Baptist church, cold enough to generate clouds and winds strong enough to send leaves scattering in every direction for a mile or more, and through it all, they hungered and seethed, impatient for a greater feast than they'd been allowed so far.

It was Halloween, or close enough that the world was already responding. The dead were restless in Wellman and they, too, were drawn to the area, like moths to a potent flame.

And though he did not have far to travel, the thing that had been Thaddeus Crawford took its time moving closer. It observed the dead and the ravenous dead alike, and if it had a proper face, it would have smiled in that moment, content in the knowledge that it would feast soon as the barriers between the realms of the living and the dead continued to break down.

Do the dead feel? Oh, yes. The dead in Wellman felt everything around them. They felt life. They tasted the essence of the living as it swirled around them in a constant miasma, and they felt the presence of death as it called to them and bade them rest when rest was beyond them.

The air in Wellman was a tempest unfelt by living beings, a storm grew above the town and raged on, unseen, unheard, as clouds gathered and winds grew stronger, reflecting the raging, howling power of the hungry dead.

The skull-phantoms were the hungry dead and they did not wait long before their endless burning hunger got the better of them. Though they were drawn to their crypt, nothing that happened there mattered as much as feasting, and so they fed, tearing at the dead, ravenous and insatiable, and as they fed, they, in turn, gave a portion of themselves to Thaddeus Crawford, whose hunger was worse than theirs could ever be. If they were candle flames, he was a forest fire of massive scale, and he burned so very brightly....

———

"Well, this blew up from the proverbial nowhere," Crowley shook his head and looked at the darkening skies above them.

"Not from nowhere," Decamp said. "The atmospheric disturbance is just a reflection of what we're up against."

"And it'll likely get worse. We need to fix this soon, Carter."

"Agreed, though I'm somewhat unclear on how."

"That's the challenge, isn't it?" Crowley shook his head. "That's the thing with hungry ghosts, they never seem to play out the same way twice. I don't think this is going to go smoothly. Just once, I'd like the town I'm trying to defend from a hungry ghost to survive the experience."

Decamp said, "I'm sure the residents of Wellman would join you in that wish."

They had almost reached the entrance to the church when three figures came barreling through the front doors and down the stairs. Travis, Emily, and Sascha, running as if the very hounds of hell pursued them. Perhaps they did.

"Travis!" Decamp said. "Are you all right?"

"Decamp. Jesus, am I glad to see you. We found the crypt where Crawford is buried. I don't think he's happy about it."

Crowley said, "He wouldn't be. There's still a chance that he has a connection to his physical remains. If he does, that's a stroke of luck for us."

Decamp nodded his head and asked, "Can you tell us where the bodies are hidden?"

Sascha answered. "We can show you."

The winds howled loudly enough that Decamp had to wait a moment before he could respond. "Best you tell us and run. I think we're about to have a very bad situation on our hands."

Above them the storm clouds swirled and, somewhere in the darkness, Thaddeus Crawford watched as his acolytes gathered. He did not know the people preparing to face him, but Nsnigoth was with him and he intended to prevail.

Travis told Decamp how to get to the hidden chamber. Decamp said, "Cindy was right about its location then. Thank you, Travis. Now the three of you need to get as far from here as possible."

"No argument here," Travis said. Then he and his two companions hurried away in the gathering storm.

———

Carter Decamp and Jonathan Crowley hurried up the steps and entered the darkened sanctuary. Brilliant flashes of lightning exploded beyond the stained-glass windows, alternating blinding light with utter darkness. They were halfway across the big room when Decamp heard the shrieking of the creatures dubbed skull-phantoms.

"Looks like they're coming home to roost," Crowley said.

Decamp said, "Can you hold them for a moment, Jonathan? I have an idea."

Crowley smiled. "If I can't, we're going to find out real sudden like."

Unbound by physical barriers, the screaming dead came flooding through the walls into the sanctuary. Their eyes blazed with fury and hunger, and their claws were extended to rend and tear.

Jonathan Crowley drew patterns in the air with his hands, speaking a guttural invocation as he did so. Decamp felt the air in the room change, and the entire chamber was filled with a baleful blue glow. The shrieking creatures hovered in the air, no longer attacking.

"I'm not going to be able to hold them for long, Carter," Crowley said.

"I'll be quick then," Decamp said. He reached into a pocket and produced a chunk of red chalk.

Decamp knelt and began making quick, sure strokes with the chalk on the sanctuary's tan carpeting. Perhaps three people in the world could have read the words he wrote there, and two of them were in the room.

As Decamp worked, the skull-phantoms became more agitated and began to writhe and twist in the air. Crowley's brow furrowed. "Carter…"

"Almost there. Hold on."

A moment later the wraiths vanished. A peal of thunder echoed through the chamber at that very moment.

Crowley grinned. "Nice work. You reunited them with their earthly remains."

Decamp nodded. "It seemed the best plan."

"Agreed, but now they're waiting on us down below."

"But they can't fly away," Decamp said. "They're bound to their bodies. At least for now."

Crowley said, "Well, let's go see what we've wrought."

―――――――――

"I have to go back," Emily said, just as Sascha unlocked her car.

Travis started at Emily. His eyes wide. "What?"

"I have to go back to the church," Emily said. "I don't know why, but I do."

Sascha said, "What are you talking about? We barely got away."

But Emily was done talking. She turned and started back the way they had come. Travis hurried after her and caught her by the arm. Emily whirled and struck Travis across the face with a resounding slap. More shocked than hurt, Travis released her and the girl took off at a dead run.

"Shit!" Travis said and ran after her.

Decamp and Crowley made their way to the basement. They paused at a wide, ragged hole in the drywall. They had expected the hidden chamber to be pitch black, but instead a weird greenish radiance poured from the opening.

Decamp, "Once more into the breach, old friend."

Crowley nodded.

Decamp drew the silver-edged blade from his walking stick and dropped the stick to the floor. Then he stepped through the hole.

A desiccated mummy came rushing at Decamp even as he entered the chamber. One of its feet was missing, but that didn't slow it down much. He knew, of course, that the figure was animated by the skull-phantom trapped within. He whipped the blade through the air, severing the mummy's head and the figure fell. Bound to the earth, the wraiths lost much of their eldritch power. He had been counting on that.

None of the other revenants were so brash. They clustered around a single figure that was considerably better preserved than the others. That figure stood there, wreathed in green flames and glaring at the two men.

"I have seen you," the flaming man said. His petrified lips didn't move, but Decamp heard his voice. "And though I don't know you, I know what you are. The mages of this modern world."

"We know you, Thaddeus Crawford," Crowley said.

"Then you know what I am becoming."

"We know what you're attempting," Decamp said.

Crawford said, "And I shall succeed. It's too late for you to stop me. My servants have brought me all the power I need. The souls of many shall carry me to godhood."

Crowley said, "You're not a god yet, Crawford, and I've faced Outer Lords before."

Decamp was aware of a rumbling from above and dust sifted down from the ceiling as the earth seemed to shake.

Crawford said, "You think to frustrate me with your wards and your incantations. I have been awake for all of my years of imprisonment. My mind has gone forth. My lord Nsnigoth has whispered to me in the eternal night. I possess knowledge you cannot imagine. Here is what I think of your wards."

The mummy of Thaddeus Crawford raised his hands and one by one his followers exploded into green fire. Corpse dust rained around the room as the walking remains were destroyed. Shrieking in triumph and hunger, the skull-phantoms rose.

Decamp gritted his teeth. Three of the creatures had almost managed to kill him. Here were a dozen eager predators. The only consolation he had was that without their physical forms to tether them to reality, any of the skull-phantoms he destroyed would be truly gone, unable to resurrect.

Crowley said, "Your turn to hold the skull-phantoms at bay, Carter. I have to keep Crawford from finishing his evolution."

"Try not to take too long, will you Jonathan?"

Crowley grinned. Light began to play about his hands as he rushed at Crawford.

The skull-phantoms whirled into the air to intercept Crowley, but Decamp rushed into their midst. From a pocket he produced a handful of what he called "conflagration dust" and threw it at the closest pair of creatures. He said a few words in an ancient tongue and the dust burst into flame.

The two wraiths screeched in pain as they were enveloped in fire. Decamp turned from them as he felt claws rake across his back. Spinning away from the attack, he lashed out with the sword, decapitating the third skull-phantom. He had succeeded too well in distracting the creatures. They had forgotten Crowley and were now determined to destroy Carter Decamp.

Decamp vaulted over one of the stone tables and landed in a wide spot on the stone floor. He put the tip of his sword against the floor and spun quickly, etching a circle in the stone, speaking a few more words in that strange language as he did so. The next skull-phantom that flew at him slammed into an invisible wall. Several others whirled around him, reaching out with their claws but found they were unable to touch him. The creatures shrieked in rage and frustration and gathered around the invisible barrier.

That was what Decamp had been waiting for. He lashed out with the sword, cutting and slashing. Though the things couldn't get to him, the barrier only worked one way. Three more of the creatures were down before the others were able to sweep back out of the reach of the sword.

Then two of the remaining skull-phantoms grasped opposite ends of one of the stone tables and flipped it at Decamp. He was forced to leave the circle of protection to avoid being crushed. Decamp backpedaled into a corner and stood at bay as the skull-phantoms whirled closer and closer.

Thaddeus Crawford's burning wraith moved slowly, almost carefully, as it stared at Jonathan Crowley. The mask half hiding Crawford's face turned slowly as he watched his prey. The funeral shroud surrounding that withered form whipped in a wind that no one else felt, and the eldritch energies of Nsnigoth offered that same sickly green glow in a corona around him.

The dead did not rest in Wellman, but in this case they feasted well.

Crowley lashed out with an incantation that would have destroyed most dead things. The energies bathed Crawford in a pure, silvery light that had the specter recoiling at the unexpected pain, but failed to end the wretched thing's existence. The protection of the Outer God was powerful, indeed.

Crawford let out a hiss of annoyance and backed away.

Crowley pushed forward, seeking to press his advantage, but Crawford struck just as fast and hard, sending a dark green bolt of energy from his skeletal fingers. The eldritch power crashed into Crowley's body with the force of a water cannon and sent him staggering. He felt his skin burn and blister, and bared his teeth in a vulpine grimace of pain.

There was no conversation. There was only attack and defense.

A furious itching sensation moved over Crowley's body. Regeneration was not a comfortable thing, but it kept him alive. Crawford reached out with withered hands and grabbed at him, long, bony fingers scraping at cloth and flesh as the dead man hissed an incantation.

Jonathan Crowley was not a normal man. He had survived many situations where a person should simply not have walked away. That was true in that moment, as well. The agony was a sudden explosion, and it felt like his bones were melting in his body. Crowley howled with pain and Crawford lunged in closer, ready to destroy his enemy.

And Crowley decked him for his efforts, striking the cadaverous face, knocking aside his funeral mask and revealing the rotted flesh hidden away. Crowley's fingers clutched at that ruin and a second later a different light burned across the funeral shroud, searing the fabric and the skin beneath it.

Crawford struck back, his hand clutching at Crowley's chest, his fingers pushing past cloth, reaching for flesh and digging, pushing to reach the beating heart of his enemy.

Crowley staggered back. Nsnigoth's power truly did move through Crawford, and even as Crowley healed, the damned wraith came for him again, seeking to destroy him and doing an admirable job of it.

Crowley lashed out with his own sorceries and the two struggled back and forth, but much as Crowley hated to admit it, the dead man seemed to have the upper hand. He was weakening, and Thaddeus Crawford was not.

And, yes, Crawford was changing. The differences were subtle so far, but Crowley had no doubt they would become more obvious as the influence of Nsnigoth, working through the dead man's form, became more blatant and potent.

The eldritch energies surrounding the specter flared and flowed and subtle ripples ran through cadaverous flesh. The eyes locked in the skeletal face burned with madness, and shriveled lips pulled back in a sadistic, victorious grin.

"I am becoming…"

"You already said that, asshole." Crowley struck again, grabbing the corpse's shoulders and doing his best to pull Crawford's remains from within the cocoon of Nsnigoth's power, but it was too late. The union of god and servant was too far along. Dead flesh shifted, mended, and regrew slowly, but it regrew.

Thaddeus Crawford reached out with a burning hand and grabbed at Crowley's face, and narrowly missed. Crowley lashed out again, striking the cadaverous jaw and having almost no effect. Normally the monsters he hit felt it.

"Enough. Time to end this." Crawford's hands caught him again and eldritch power coursed from him into Crowley, burning, igniting every nerve ending. The pain was a tidal wave that threatened to drown him, obscure his thoughts and bury him alive.

And then the girl was there. Emily. She pushed into the chamber, skittering along the wall, avoiding Decamp and the skull-phantoms as she came straight for Crowley. Her eyes were wide, her teeth were bared and she hyperventilated. She did not want to be there, and Crowley knew it by the horrified expression on her face.

"Crawford!" The voice belonged to a man, but came from the college girl's throat.

Thaddeus Crawford turned his head and his ruined face scowled in concentration. "Who is that?"

"You know me, fool!" She hissed the words as she stared at him and even as she spoke a corona of light broke around her, lighting her eyes from inside, dancing in an aura around her body, her face. She shook her head, her expression one of fear that did not match the unearthly voice emanating from her.

In the broken doorway, the young man, Travis, who was so enamored with Emily, watched on, staring, frozen in place by what he saw in the chamber he had so recently fled with Emily and Sascha.

Emily stepped forward and her hand reached like a striking cobra, clutched at Crawford's arm, held on tight as the energies around her boiled forth and lashed into Thaddeus Crawford. The air around Crawford crackled and hissed and Emily was thrown back as whatever it was residing in her was unleashed. The girl fell back, staggered by whatever had left her body. Travis hurried to her side.

Crowley suspected that the restless spirit of William Avery Harrington wanted revenge for what had been done to him by Crawford and his associates. He had never met the man, but he'd felt enough of his presence to believe the dead sought vengeance and would have it.

Somehow the spirit had hidden within the girl, using her as a way to reach Crawford undetected.

Crawford hissed and groaned as an aura of silvery light danced across his body like an electrical charge. The revenant's skin burned anew, and the slowly changing flesh of the thing burned in that light, smoldered as if threatening to catch fire. Crawford struggled to withstand the sudden onslaught, and Jonathan Crowley grinned.

Nsnigoth wanted back into the world, but the world did not want the Outer Ones to return. That was simple math in Crowley's book. The world had moved on and continued to change, to evolve, while ancient forces wished for stagnation or destruction. Life fought to live.

Crowley aimed to help it.

He cast his incantation quickly, as the reanimated corpse of Thaddeus Crawford fought to wrest itself away from the spirit of Harrington. Dead flesh erupted in cleansing fire and Crowley grinned again as he backed away, the light from the fire as brilliant as the noon day sun in the chamber where Crawford and his minions had rested while waiting for their time to finally come.

Not far away Carter Decamp suddenly found himself without opponents. The spirits of Crawford's minions were released from their service, whether they wanted that release or not. Without bodies to return to they dissipated, burned by the same cleansing fire that tore through Crawford's mortal remains.

Nsnigoth's influence was severed as his servant's body, long prepared for the moment of ascension, burned brighter still and crumbled into little more than ash.

Thaddeus Crawford screamed as he burned, denied the immortality he had sought for so very long, and prepared himself for as he awaited the blessings of his uncaring god.

In moments it was over. Crowley reached out with his mind and hands alike and caught the disembodied spirit of Thaddeus Crawford. It writhed and burned against him, the energies searing his flesh as if he'd shoved his hands into a pit of hot coals. Even now the bastard refused to die easily.

"Little help here, please, Carter."

"Gladly," said Carter Decamp, stepping forward. He thrust his silver-edged blade into the spectral thing that was all that remained of Thaddeus Crawford.

Jonathan Crowley did not know this history of the sword and did not need to know. It was enough to understand that the blade worked as well as any exorcism and either destroyed the spirit or cast it into another realm.

Crowley and Decamp stood among the wreckage of the hidden chamber. The room had gone suddenly silent. That silence was broken by the sound of Travis's voice.

"Is it over?" Travis said.

"It's over," said Crowley. He glanced over to where the young man knelt next to the fallen girl. "How's Emily?"

Travis shook his head. "I don't know. She's breathing, but she's still unconscious. I need to get her out of here."

Decamp stepped over to the couple. He leaned down and placed his hand at Emily's throat. "Her pulse is strong. She'll be fine, Travis. But yes, let's get her out of here."

"Yes, let's," Crowley said. "Won't be long before the authorities arrive."

———

On a cold day in early November, Travis, Emily, and Sascha stood at the grave of Don Washington. They had attended the funeral the day before, but now they had come to pay their respects in private. Mark hadn't been at the funeral, and he still wasn't answering anyone's calls.

Travis said, "Maybe Mark has the right idea. I want to distance myself from all of this, but I felt like I had to come this last time."

Emily said. "Me too. Don was an idiot, but he was our idiot."

Sascha said, "I still can't believe all of this. It's going to take a long time to process all that happened. I feel like we should dedicate the book to Don."

Travis said, "You're still going through with the book?"

"I have to," Sascha said. "Now more than ever. We've seen the supernatural is real. I feel like I need to let people know."

"People aren't going to believe you," Emily said.

Sascha said, "It doesn't matter. I still have to do it."

Travis heard a car door shut and he turned to see Carter Decamp walking toward them. Behind him, gray clouds hurried across a pewter colored sky.

When he reached the group, Decamp said, "I'm glad to find you three here. I couldn't come to the funeral, so I came to pay my respects."

"We appreciate it, Decamp," Travis said. "What about Mr. Crowley?"

Decamp said, "Jonathan has already left town. He doesn't tend to linger once a situation has been resolved."

Emily said, "He's a scary man."

Decamp said, "He can be. But he has his reasons."

Sascha said, "I saw on the news the authorities are saying a tornado hit the Baptist church. There wasn't anything about the hidden chamber."

Decamp said, "There wouldn't be. The ceiling conveniently collapsed, burying everything under tons of rubble."

"Did the ceiling have any help in collapsing?" Travis said.

"That would be telling," said Decamp. "In any case, I've done what damage control I can. I advise all of you to keep a low profile for a while. The police don't have anything to directly link any of you to the events, but they haven't forgotten you and Mark were at the farm, Sascha."

Travis said, "I don't plan to ever talk about this again if I can help it."

"Probably best. But if you should ever need to, feel free to call me."

"Thanks, Decamp," Travis said.

Emily said, "My memory of what happened in the secret room is pretty messed up. What did happen down there, Carter?"

Decamp said, "As cliched as it sounds, my dear, in this case, the less you know, the better. Crawford had aligned himself with dark entities. Dangerous beings, completely inimical to humanity. Even speaking their names might draw their attention, and we don't want that, believe me."

Emily said, "I guess you're right. I should just try and forget it happened. Well, thank you for everything, Carter."

Decamp said, "All of you take care."

With that Decamp turned and started back toward his car. Travis watched him go. Then he looked at Emily. "Are you ready to go too?"

Emily nodded. "Yes, I guess we've said everything that needs saying. Sascha?"

"You two go ahead. I want to stay here for a while."

Travis took Emily's hand and they left Sascha alone with the dead. Together they walked from the graveyard, and this time, neither one of them looked back.

About the Authors

JAMES A. MOORE authored more than forty novels. The first decades of his career focused on his love for horror, as seen in many novels including the critically acclaimed *Fireworks*, *Under the Overtree*, *Blood Red*, and the Serenity Falls trilogy. Later, Jim earned a reputation as the "prince of grimdark fantasy" with his hugely popular Seven Forges series as well as the Tides of War trilogy. The author loved collaborating with other writers, most frequently with Christopher Golden on the Bloodstained Worlds trilogy and with Charles R. Rutledge on the Griffin & Price series, among others. Nominated for the Bram Stoker Award twice, Moore won the Shirley Jackson Award for co-editing *The Twisted Book of Shadows*. He first came to prominence as one of the principal world-builders involved in the World of Darkness from White Wolf Games, most famously Vampire: The Masquerade and Werewolf: The Apocalypse. At the time of his passing, Moore left behind one completed solo fantasy novel, as well as completed collaborations with Charles R. Rutledge and Mary SanGiovanni. Plans are afoot to bring those to readers soon.

Bibliography

NOVELS

The Black Stone Bay Series
Blood Red (with "Blood Tide"
Blood Harvest
Bloodlines

The Bloodstained Series (w/Christopher Golden)
Bloodstained Oz
Bloodstained Wonderland
Bloodstained Neverland

The Chris Corin Series
Possessions
Newbies
Rabid Growth

The Chronicles of Jonathan Crowley
Under the Overtree
Writ in Blood: Serenity Falls, Book One
The Pack: Serenity Falls, Book Two
Dark Carnival: Serenity Falls, Book Three
Cherry Hill
Smile No More
Boomtown
One Bad Week
Where the Sun Goes to Die
The Tourist's Guide to Haunted Wellman (w/Charles Rutledge)

The Griffin & Price Series (w/Charles Rutledge)
Blind Shadows
Congregations of the Dead
A Hell Within

The Seven Forges Series
Seven Forges
The Blasted Lands
City of Wonders
The Silent Army
The Godless
The War Born

The Subject Seven Series
Subject Seven
Run

The Tides of War Series
The Last Sacrifice
Fallen Gods
Gates of the Dead

Standalone Novels
Deeper
Fireworks
Harvest Moon
The Haunted Forest Tour (w/ Jeff Strand)

NOVELLAS
Dear Diary: Run Like Hell
Homestead
The Wild Hunt

SHORT STORY COLLECTIONS
Slices
This is Halloween

CHARLES R. RUTLEDGE is the author of the novel *Dracula's Return*, and co-author of three novels in the Griffin and Price series, written with James A. Moore. Charles' short stories have appeared in over 50 anthologies, including *Clickers Forever*, *The Drive-in Multiplex*, and *Weird Tales*. He is the co-editor of anthologies for several publishers, including Pavane Press and Twisted Publishing. He is currently working on a collection of all the short stories and novellas he co-authored with James A. Moore.

NOVELS

The Griffin & Price Series (w/James A. Moore
Blind Shadows
Congregations of the Dead
A Hell Within

The Jennifer Grail/Carter Decamp series
Dracula's Return

The Tourist's Guide to Haunted Wellman

NOVELLAS
What Rough Beast (w/James A. Moore)
Call up the Dead (w/James A. Moore)
Dracula's Revenge
Dracula's Ghost
Virgin Zombie

Curious about other Crossroad Press books? Stop by our website:
http://crossroadpress.com
We offer quality writing
in digital, audio, and print formats.

Subscribe to our newsletter on the website homepage and receive a free
eBook.

www.ingramcontent.com/pod-product-compliance
Lightning Source LLC
Chambersburg PA
CBHW020638180626
46816CB00003B/1019